BEARTOOTH

ALSO BY CALLAN WINK

Dog Run Moon: Stories

August: A Novel

BEARTOOTH

CALLAN WINK

S&G

Spiegel & Grau, New York
www.spiegelandgrau.com

Interior design by Meighan Cavanaugh

Library of Congress Cataloging-in-Publication Data Available Upon Request

ISBN (hardcover) 978-1-954118-02-7
ISBN (eBook) 978-1-954-118-41-6

First Edition
10 9 8 7 6 5 4 3 2 1

BEARTOOTH

THAD HAD JUST SHOT A BLACK BEAR OUT OF SEASON. It was a small yearling sow, and the rancid stink of it settled like a fog over the clearing where it died. The smell of a bear, Thad thought, had the flavor of nightmare about it. Putrefying flesh, fresh shit, all held together with something cloying and sweet, like smashed huckleberries just starting to ferment. This was the third one they'd killed this week, and Thad figured they could start heading home. Three heads attached to three pelts, twelve paws, three gallbladders, on top of all their other gear—it was going to be a backbreaking hump over the mountain. He and his brother, Hazen, were twenty miles from the logging road where their truck waited, a cooler in the back with a block of ice and a twelve-pack of Coors. Just thinking of the beer made Thad swallow reflexively.

Hazen was over at the edge of the timber splashing around in a small creek that looped through a stand of alders and meandered across the clearing. It was late summer, the grass was long and dry, and the creek running through it looked like a crooked part in a shock of thick blond hair.

"Quit messing around. When we get this one cut up, we're out of here," Thad said.

"There's trout."

"We're not fishing. Get over here. I'd like to be home tomorrow morning."

Hazen stomped out of the creek. Thad could hear him grumbling as he set to work. Although he tended to stray from the task at hand, Thad had to admit that his brother was faster at butchering than he was. Hazen could break down an animal so quick it was almost unnatural. It was like he had some strange elemental knowledge of how the parts all fit together. Sometimes he didn't even use his knife. Just got the cut started and then used his hands and fingernails to divide muscles and separate flesh from bone. Thad had seen him using his teeth to snap a particularly stubborn ligament or tendon.

Thad was a year older, but they could almost pass for twins. They had the same lanky arms and legs. They weren't really all that tall, although there was something about their proportions that made them look like short men who'd been stretched. A couple years ago, Thad had started growing his hair out and Hazen had copied him. They now had shoulder-length brown ponytails that they tied back with thin strips of tanned deer hide. They both had veins that stood out in stark relief on their forearms. Their front teeth protruded slightly. It was only side by side that the differences between them became noticeable. Hazen was an inch shorter, his hair a shade lighter. His laugh came quick and stayed a beat too long. Thad was twenty-seven, Hazen twenty-six, and already they had crow's feet at the corners of their eyes. Over the years these marks would only deepen, their gazes hardening into perpetual squints. Their father's visage had been cast this way, and his father before him. Theirs were faces made for the weather, for looking into it. Hatchet chins, angled cheekbones, faces around which the high-country wind could pass with minimal resistance. Though they possessed no great strength, the men in their line had been shaped—by environment and circumstance—for tremendous acts of myopic endurance.

As Thad watched, Hazen made a quick incision up the bear's rounded gut and then plunged in up to his elbows, the bloody butt of his knife clenched between his teeth like a stogie. The gallbladder on a small black bear like this one was about the size of a golf ball. Hazen could find and excise this organ by feel, his face pointed up and away, his eyes closed with concentration, his hands moving around the hot insides of the animal as if he were rummaging through a junk drawer. Thad hadn't the slightest idea what function a gallbladder performed inside the body. Humans had one, too, he was pretty sure. All he knew was that one of decent size would go for fifteen hundred dollars, and fifteen hundred dollars was the equivalent of a half a dozen cords of firewood, cut, split, stacked, and delivered. If they wanted to be efficient, he knew that they should just go for the gallbladders and leave the rest of the animal where it lay. For the skull and the claws and the skin they could get another four or five hundred dollars, decent money until you factored in the weight and additional time it took to skin one. He knew it made no logical sense, but the extra effort and risk involved in keeping the other bear parts did something to move the whole enterprise slightly closer to hunting, something respectable. Before this trip he'd visited the computer at the library to look up likely punishments if they were to get caught. Maybe that hadn't been a good idea. As far as he could tell, what they were involved in was considered wanton waste, a severe violation of the Lacey Act, punishable by fines of up to one hundred thousand dollars. Guaranteed felonies, potential jail time.

It was easier to think that in a wilderness area this large, a person could get away with whatever he wanted, but Thad knew that wasn't true. How many times had they been deep in the backcountry only to come across a troop of Eagle Scouts from Cincinnati, a crunchy honeymooning couple, a Forest Service trail crew? It was a large wilderness area, but all sorts of people were drawn to it for that very reason. All it would take was one Sierra Club member working on his life list with a Sibley's and a pair of binoculars and they'd be completely screwed.

Across the clearing, Hazen was pulling the hide off the bear, the skin separating from the carcass with a sound like tape being pulled off a roll. He'd gotten in the habit of carrying a spent .22 shell casing in his mouth, and now he was pursing his lips to blow air over it, making the chirruping bird whistle he did when he was concentrating. Eventually Thad went to help. The quicker this got done, the quicker they could get the hell out of there, collect their money, and put this whole thing behind them.

IT TOOK THEM LONGER TO GET BACK TO THE TRUCK than Thad had anticipated. They were moving over rough ground, staying off the trails to avoid people. Thad leaned into the weight of his pack and squinted up at Hazen making his way through the slabs of rocks above him. They stopped for a breather in a large boulder field hemmed in by dark stands of spruce. The boulders were massive, dark and lichen spotted, shot through with quartzite veins. Glacial remnants, they cropped up in the grassy slope in a random scattering as if they were cast there, rugged dice thrown and left by wagering giants. They shrugged off their packs and sat on a low table of rock and looked back down the valley. It seemed like they'd come a long way, but Thad could still see the ridge that hid the small meadow where he'd killed the bear. A full day's hike away and it looked like he could throw a rock to it. Right now, Thad figured they had a hard half a day's walk left before they dropped back down to the truck. They had at least three ridges to cross, give or take, and they'd be back to civilization, back to showers and beer and everything else. Thad leaned back against his pack and spit. "We're getting there," he said.

Hazen didn't respond. He was watching the little gray forms of the pikas scurrying around in the rocks, letting loose their shrill warning calls. He held the .22 casing sideways between his teeth and blew sharp puffs of air across its rim, creating a set of piercing whistles. Hazen was smiling, his cheeks rounded out and his eyes slightly crossed as he concentrated on the blowing. "Ha," he said. "How about that? I'm speaking pika. Look at those little shits."

There were half a dozen pikas flitting back and forth on the rocks, darting from one side to the other, stopping occasionally to turn and shake their stubby tails. Clearly, they were incensed at this gigantic imposter mangling their language. Hazen kept up with the call and searched around on the ground next to him with one hand, not taking his eyes off the rodents. When he found a suitable rock, he threw it, sending them scurrying off.

Eventually Thad heaved to his feet and they started out again. During their stop the sun had reached the high point of the day and begun its slow slide west. Even up in the high country, it still had the power to heat you up. It was behind them now, and Thad could feel the warmth of its gaze on the back of his neck; he could smell the bearskin heating up under the tarp strapped to the pack frame. It was like hiking with a festering compost pile on his back, everything overripe and hot with the fever of decomposition.

It took almost a mile to lose the flies that had found them when they had stopped. They buzzed around Thad's head, not biting but still an annoyance, especially as they scrambled across a shifting scree slope where a misstep would mean sliding fifty yards or more down the mountain. Hazen led them on meandering elk and deer trails. Sometimes they veered off at random, cross-country, through rock falls and tangled labyrinths of blown-down timber, until they linked up with another game trail that kept them headed back in their intended direction—toward the truck.

They'd ditched most of their food and water to make room for the additional bear parts, and they'd had nothing substantial to eat for almost twenty-four hours. Thad could feel himself weakening. Under the weight of the pack his spine felt like it was being compressed and permanently fused. He thought that when he finally removed the pack he'd remain hunched, his back forced into a tortured question mark. Roots and rocks reached out and grabbed at his feet. Uphill climbs that hours ago would have barely given him pause caused him to puff and blow, his legs screaming from the effort. His mouth was starting to dry out, his tongue sticking to his gums, his teeth covered in a paste that made his upper lip pull back in a perpetual grimace. Eventually, he came around a bend in the deer trail and found Hazen down on his hands and knees, his pack still on, splashing water over his face. They were down in the bed of a small creek, now mostly dry, with just a trickle purling over white sand and rocks made oval and brilliant by the wet vein of water. Thad found a small declivity where the water poured over a flat rock and collected into a sink-basin-sized pool. He flopped down on his belly, submerging his head entirely, sucking great draughts of water, his eyes open to the effervescent swirl of bubbles rising from the plunge. He drank until pinpricks of white light danced around behind his eyes and he had to break for air. The water tasted of moss and stone. A silkiness on the tongue that water from the tap never seemed to possess.

Refreshed, they hiked. And when the sun fell below the peaks behind them, they kept going through the murky half-light, the shapes of things softened in the gloom, the smell of the pines turning damp as the air cooled. As full dark descended, Hazen led them through a stand of aspen, and they picked their way through the trees. The trunks gathered the moonlight, glowed silver. The aspen leaves had already started to turn, just showing a hint of gold at the edges, and it wouldn't be long before the snow fell up here, great drifts of it shape-shifting in the wind, forming ridges like wave troughs on the lee sides of the trees. When Thad ran his fingers over the smooth bark of the aspens, it seemed like they exuded warmth, released the heat they'd stored up during the day. He thought aspens could be spooky trees. They liked their own company, grew up close so their leaves could touch one another and their branches could reach together and intertwine like fingers. His father had told him once how the biggest organism in the world was a stand of aspen trees in Canada that stretched for a thousand miles. When you came upon a grove of aspens, you weren't walking through separate life-forms. Aspens are clones; they send up shoots from their shared root mass, so a whole stand of trees might be one plant, the separate trees separate only in the way that a man's foot is separate from his hand. Thad didn't know exactly how to explain it, but he thought that, as a group, aspens had a sort of consciousness.

This particular stand of trees seemed to stretch forever, but when he finally broke out into a clearing, he could see the overgrown trailhead in the distance, and there was Hazen dumping his pack beside the wheels of their truck.

Only a sliver of ice remained in the cooler, but the beer was so cold it made the back of his throat ache. Thad downed half a bottle in one gulp and then released a prodigious belch. He'd stashed a bag of elk jerky in the truck, and they ripped and chewed the salty meat until their jaws hurt, washing it down with the beer, belching and yawning and stretching their arms and backs. They sat on the dropped tailgate, and Thad decided that instead of driving the maze of logging roads in the dark, they should just camp out one more night, handle the transaction out here in the woods tomorrow, and then head home after all the contraband had been transferred.

"I'm going to start a fire." Hazen rummaged around in the cooler for another beer. He'd had four already, about as many as Thad ever liked him to have. Something about booze made Hazen argumentative, less pliant than he normally was.

"No fire. And you're done after that one. Find a spot to crash. Take your pack with you; don't leave it in the truck."

"My sleeping bag is wet. I'm going to start a fire and dry it out."

"Why is your bag wet?"

"I don't know, it just is."

"Well, that's your own stupid fault. It's not that cold anyway; you'll be fine. You could have been airing it out this whole time instead of bitching and drinking all my beer."

"If I can't have a fire then at least let me have another beer." He had finished his last one in three long drinks, half-chewed jerky still in his mouth.

"No fire. No more beer. Find a spot to crash, and I'll see you in the morning."

"That's bullshit. One more beer. I'll pay you back."

"No."

"Why?"

"You know why. Go sleep."

Hazen took one more piece of jerky and reached for the cooler. Thad chopped his wrist down, and then Hazen slid from the tailgate and stomped off into the dark, dragging his pack behind him. Thad could hear the sound of breaking branches, incoherent muttering. Thad got himself another beer and reclined against his foul-smelling pack and yawned. Hazen could be a royal pain in the ass. He probably should just forbid him from drinking at all.

Last year Thad had to pull him out from under a pack of firefighters who were intent on rearranging his face. He'd gotten a call from the bartender at the Blue Goose, who said he should probably get over there quick before Hazen got his neck broken. By the time he arrived, Hazen had already talked his way into a pretty sizable ass beating. It was a small town, and no local would have let Hazen get under his skin, but it was late summer, and there were wildfires burning all over in the mountains. Town was full of hotshot crews from down south. Thad never did find out exactly what Hazen had said. When he got to the bar, three short, wide, Mexican-looking dudes were about to start applying their three-hundred-dollar White's to Hazen's skinny midsection. Luckily Thad had been able to pull Hazen out and smooth things over. He bought drinks. He wasn't sure if the men spoke English. He pointed at Hazen and tapped his head, spiraling his finger around his ear. "Loco," he said.

If he never had to go to town, Hazen would be just fine, Thad figured. Hell, during some era not too far past, Hazen would have probably been happier and more well-adjusted than Thad. He could have trapped, lived in the woods, got royally drunk once a year at some sort of mountain-man rendezvous, and spent the next year working off his hangover, alone in the mountains, skinning beaver and talking to himself.

Another beer. Thad was more comfortable than he'd been in days. He couldn't even smell himself anymore. He knew he'd been out in the woods for a while when the scent of his unwashed body no longer smelled foreign. He adjusted his position so he could look up. There was a narrow strip of clear sky, a scattering of stars, hemmed in by banks of purple-gray clouds. They'd lucked out with the weather this trip, nothing but blue skies. Rain in the backcountry made everything more difficult. The narrow logging roads would turn to gumbo, tracks were obliterated, and, more than anything, the basic dampness would slowly wear him down. Dry socks seemed like a small thing until the fourth or fifth day of waking up in the mud to put on wet socks before cramming his feet back into sodden boots.

Thad finished the last beer and struggled to his feet to piss, sending a glorious stream out over the edge of the truck bed into the darkness, the sound of it faintly musical against the leaf-littered ground. He was fairly drunk. He dragged his pack off into the stand of aspens and right up against the base of a tree, then cleared a small area free of sticks and rocks. He removed the tarp from around the bearskin and laid it out. He spread his bedroll on top and crawled in—not even removing his boots—and folded the tarp over him. It smelled like he'd rolled himself up in a pile of warm bear intestine.

AT SOME POINT IN THE NIGHT THAD CAME AWAKE. THERE was a glow coming through the trees, the sound of fire crackling. He kicked out of his bedroll and walked gingerly, barefoot, through the brush until he could see what it was: a spruce about fifteen feet tall, completely consumed by flames. The fire was like a glowing orange-red aura, and at its very core the tree's skeleton was still visible, the skinny black trunk, the spindly limbs radiating out like spokes on a wheel. The tree was popping, the cones exploding like shots, sparks spiraling up into the dark sky against the spitting rain.

Hazen stood there slack-jawed like he did when he didn't know anyone was watching him. He had his shirt off. In his boots and blood-stained jeans, hair loose around his face, his arms spread to the tree as if he were offering it an embrace, Hazen rotated slowly so his bare back was to the fire. He had his eyes closed and his mouth open and his head tilted back. He was warming himself. Close enough to the flames that the heat made his hair rise, as if consumed with static.

Thad emerged from the timber walking slowly and quietly. Hazen's eyes were still closed, and Thad got right up on him. This close to the tree the fire was loud, a dull continuous rush, like wind across a lake. It was the sound of the tree, moments earlier a living thing, being transferred into something else entirely. The tree's needles were either black and curled up like singed hair or glowing molten red like the filaments in an overheated incandescent light bulb. Thad could feel his skin prickle with the heat. The air smelled of the bubbling pitch leaking from the tree's white-hot trunk. Thad stood two feet in front of Hazen, and he raised back his arm, his hand open, to deliver the most earth-shattering slap he could muster. And then, just before he brought it down, Hazen smiled widely.

"Howdy," he said. "I bet you're pissed." He'd obviously known Thad was there the whole time. Thad still had his arm raised back and he wanted more than anything to drop the hammer, to just obliterate that stupid smile from Hazen's stupid face. He lowered his hand and tilted his head back and let a few raindrops pelt him in the face. "What in the hell?"

"I don't know. I was cold. My bag was wet. I was thinking about totem poles. I always thought that burned-up pine trees looked like totem poles that someone just carved on too much or made mistakes that they had to erase, that's why they're all smooth."

"I tell you not to light a fire and you decide to burn down the whole fucking woods?"

"It's just one tree. It was starting to die. Half its needles were brown."

"What if the wind picked up? Do you think? Ever?"

"Everything's wet. I don't think anything else will burn. It took me a long time to get this one going. Actually, I didn't think it would be that hard. If I'd have known it was going to take that long I probably wouldn't have bothered."

Thad thought it was like training a dog. A dumb, hardheaded mongrel. You couldn't punish a dog for something it couldn't understand. All that did was make the animal fear you, make it more likely to bite. They stood and watched the tree burn, the flames pushing up against the black roof of clouds.

"Jesus," Thad said eventually. "That's like twenty, thirty feet high, at least."

"It reminds me of the World Trade Center. Remember watching that?"

"When the buildings collapsed?"

"Not that. After, when they shot those big beams of light up in the sky where the buildings used to be. That's why I did it; I thought it might look like that. A memorial for dad."

"I thought you wanted to make a totem pole."

"That too."

"Or were you just cold?

"That too."

"Great. Well, we have to move pretty soon now. I don't know if the fire lookouts are manned this time of year, but you've pretty much made our presence known to anyone in a five-mile radius. If someone is up in a lookout, they've probably called it in already."

The raging fire was already starting to falter; great swaths of smoke pulsed like breath exhaled on a cold morning. As the flames began to subside, Thad could see that most of the tree's needles remained attached. They were curled and brittle but still there, like the tree had just flash-aged.

Thad moved in and gave the tree a kick with the heel of his boot. It was enough to cause all the needles to shatter into particles of ash, which drifted around them like dirty snow.

"Get your pack," he said. "We're getting out of here. You're lucky I don't punch you more often."

THE SKY WAS JUST STARTING TO GET LIGHT IN THE EAST as they loaded up. False dawn. The sun wouldn't be up for an hour. They had the bear skins and skulls and parts in the truck bed covered in tarps, over which they'd stacked a small load of cut lodgepoles. If anyone asked, they were up getting new fence posts for their corral. Hazen had thought this was an unnecessary precaution.

"We don't even have a corral. And there's no one out here anyway," Hazen said. "You ever think about how the world could end sometime when you're out in the backcountry and you'd never know? New York City could have been taken out by a bomb. We might be the only people in the country that don't know about it."

"Could be. Take this; let me know when we have a signal." Thad handed Hazen his phone and took a turn that led up the mountain.

Thad parked the truck in an open clearing and got out to make the call. When the arrangements were made, directions given, he got back in the truck.

"They'll be here in an hour," he said. "I'm going to take a nap. You are going to keep an eye out and wake me up when they get here."

"Is it the Scot?"

"What do you think?"

"I just need to know who to look out for, that's all."

"It's the same as before. Why would it be any different?"

"Think she'll be with him?"

"She's always with him. Now shut up and let me sleep."

Thad leaned his head against the window. He didn't feel like he'd slept, but he must have, because he came awake to Hazen rapping on the other side of the window. His face inches from the glass, he was gesturing down the road.

"OK," Thad said, groggily. "Jesus, I'm awake." He looked in the rearview mirror and could see a black Suburban with oversized tires coming up the road. Vanity plates that read HILANDR. He got the rifle from behind the seat and pulled the bolt to make sure it was loaded. He got out and stretched and leaned against the side of the truck with the muzzle of the rifle in his palm, the butt resting on his boot.

"We'll do it like last time," he said. "You give him the packs. I'll talk. Just do what I tell you."

Hazen nodded and jammed his hands down in his pockets and gave himself a shake, rolling his neck as if he were a boxer getting ready to enter the ring.

"Just relax. Nothing different from last time. We'll get this done and get a shower. A burger."

"OK. Sure. I'm cool." Hazen bounced on his toes and tucked his hair back behind his ears. "I'm good."

The Suburban crawled up next to them and then executed a slow Y-turn in the narrow road. It backed up so its rear bumper was in line with their truck's tailgate. The Suburban had dark tinted windows, and its long black sides were spackled with red mud. Hazen whistled, nervously, as the Scot opened his door and got out.

The Scot had killed. Two years ago, the Scot had shot a sixteen-year-old boy four times in the back in his living room. Everyone in town knew it, and he knew everyone in town knew it, and that knowledge seemed to nourish his existence. Thad thought it was a strong position to be in, to know with some degree of certainty what everyone who saw you was thinking. The story was that the Scot had come home, in the dark, with his daughter, to find someone trying to break into his gun safe. He put four hollow-point bullets in the burglar's back, sent his daughter up to her room, and then called the police to report a break-in. The kid was known around town. Somewhat of a troublemaker but not necessarily a bad kid. There were those in town who thought the Scot was justified and those who thought the Scot was a trigger-happy maniac who was just looking for an excuse. In the end, the Scot was cleared of all charges. The boy was found to have had a small amount of pot on him. A knife. It was ruled a drug-fueled breaking and entering, to which the Scot was well within his rights to respond with lethal force.

Thad had met the kid once or twice. He'd been a pretty good football player and then got kicked off the team halfway through his sophomore year. Thad had gone to high school with his sister.

Now the Scot walked toward them, a smile on his big raw-boned face. He was unusually tall, closer to seven feet than six. There were rumors that he'd been on a professional basketball team in the seventies. His kilt was red-and-black highland plaid. He wore tall wool socks and black thick-soled boots. A white button-down dress shirt tucked into the kilt, a thin black tie with a tie clip shaped like a thistle. He wore his pistol in a shoulder holster, and it looked small there against his massive frame, a toy pistol.

The Scot was weathered in a way that made determining his age impossible; he looked younger than sixty-five, older than forty. His hands always reminded Thad of those huge hairy tropical spiders, the kind that are the size of dinner plates and hunt birds. He had a shock of red hair going gray at the temples. His arms were long and still corded with muscle, his joints too big, hard and gnarled like abnormal growths in dense hardwood.

"Boys," he said. "I can smell you from here. You smell like absolute shit." He smiled. "But that's OK. Smells like money. Hunting was good?"

"Show him, Hazen."

Hazen pulled the packs from under the lodgepoles and spread the skins, heads and claws still attached, for the Scot's approval.

He nodded and said they looked fine, and Hazen quickly rolled them back in the tarps.

"How about organs?"

Hazen held up the gallon Ziplocs with the gallbladders smashed together and the Scot took the bags and rolled them around in his hands, counting. "Just think of how many fine boners these will occasion," he said, smiling. "Darling," he said over his shoulder, "would you come and bring that envelope with you?"

The Scot's daughter climbed out of the passenger seat and came to stand next to her father. Though she was as slight as he was large, like her father, it was hard to discern her age. She could have been fifteen years old or in her early twenties. The Scot put a hand on her head, his hairy fingers coming down on her forehead like fat caterpillars. It was strange, Thad thought, not the way you would think a father would rest his hand on his daughter's head. Less a display of affection and more a method of keeping a hold on a skittish animal. The girl wore Carhartt overalls and a green knit stocking cap from under which two auburn braids protruded. She held a bank envelope. Thad didn't like that the Scot always involved her in the proceedings. There was no logical reason for her presence, but there she was. As Thad watched, the Scot gave her head a squeeze and a push. She walked over and handed the envelope to Thad. He opened it and thumbed through the bills, propping the rifle against his leg as he did. He motioned for Hazen to start loading the packs.

When the transaction was done, the Scot extended his hand to Hazen, who shook it quickly, not looking up from the ground, and then disentangled his hand abruptly, as if he'd grabbed on to something hot. "Good man," said the Scot. He looked to Thad and made a motion like a handshake in his direction. Thad nodded, raising the envelope of money.

"Pleasure doing business with you," the Scot said, squinting slightly into the sun, kneading his daughter's head with one of his massive hands. "OK, then. I just had a thought. Are you boys in a hurry?"

Thad said that they should probably get going, but the Scot ignored him.

The Scot looked down at his daughter. "Darling, how about a tune? It's good for you to play for someone other than me. Get your pipes. These boys look like they could use some culture."

"Right on," Hazen said.

Thad spit and jammed the envelope in his back pocket. The Scot's daughter came back from the front of the Suburban with a small set of bagpipes slung over her shoulder, the pipes sticking up above her head, stiff and spindly as the legs of a dead fawn. She stood and looked expectantly at the Scot, who shrugged and said, "'Amazing Grace'?"

The girl took a deep breath, and her cheeks bulged out as she filled the bag with air. A drone came from the pipes, sounding like a swarm of bees, and then came the first few bars of "Amazing Grace." The girl's face was red with effort, and she walked a short little path as she played, taking three steps, turning, and retracing her walk, then repeating. Her fingers moved over the pipes wildly; her eyes were clamped shut in concentration, a small magical being in the process of incantation. Hazen was staring with an open mouth. Thad had to admit it was pretty good. And loud. It was surprising how much noise the girl was able to produce, the sound of the pipes echoing and reverberating off the rocks, the music seeming to come from all directions at once.

The Scot listened with his eyes closed, a small frown on his craggy face. When the girl finished, air leaked from the pipes with a dying wheeze. Hazen clapped wildly. The Scot clapped as well, and he looked at Thad with narrowed eyes until Thad made a show of patting his leg with his left hand. His right hand was still curled around the rifle barrel.

"It seems that you have fans," the Scot said. "Now go put your pipes away and sit in the truck. I want to talk to these boys for a minute, and then we'll be leaving." When the Suburban door slammed, the Scot rubbed his face with his hands. "Music is how God celebrates the world he created," he said. And then, "How do you boys feel about antlers?"

"Antlers?" said Hazen.

"How do you mean?" said Thad.

"I could sell as many elk antlers as I could possibly get my hands on. At a good price too. If I had a mountain of elk antlers, I could move them in a day. Chandeliers. That's what's doing it. There's an Amish guy making these chandeliers and selling them up in Big Sky. Everyone wants one. Chandeliers the size of flying saucers. Cost is no issue, really. He's struggling to get the product."

"An Amish guy?" Hazen said.

"Too bad for the Amish guy," Thad said. "But it's too hard, and not worth the time. It's either shoot the animal, which is a pain in the ass, and out of the question if you need numbers. Or find the sheds, which is like finding a needle in a haystack out here. We find a few every year, but altogether they'd amount to a pretty small chandelier."

"I know where there's lots of them." Hazen had hopped up on the tailgate of the truck and was swinging his feet. "Most of them around here winter in one area; you just have to go there. That's where they drop their antlers."

"Shut up, Hazen. That's not an option."

"I'm just saying that there are tons of them there, as many as you could ever want. Just sitting there."

"What's the problem?" the Scot said. "Is it on private property? You two don't strike me as individuals who spend much time in contemplation of property rights." He smoothed the front of his kilt, a gesture Thad found to be strangely feminine, like a secretary who had just risen from two hours at the desk.

"It's in Yellowstone," Hazen said. "They're all over the place when you get back in there a ways."

"Get in the truck. We're done here," Thad said.

"Geez. Fine. I was just saying." Hazen slid off the tailgate and got in the cab, slamming the door behind him.

"Well, why not?" said the Scot. "If there's as many as he says, seems like it would be easy. If you got me two truckloads, maybe a hundred of them, I'd give you almost what I gave you today. A day's work."

"Nope," Thad said, opening his door. "It's federal there. You can't so much as pick a flower or take home a piece of petrified wood. Too many rangers, too many tourists. Not going to happen.

They put microchips in antlers in the park. Did you know that? They put GPS devices in the antlers and then plant them out where someone will see them and pick them up, and then when they do they get a visit from the Park Service the next day. That's a felony. To hell with that. This was our last hunt. We're done."

"Microchips? Are you kidding me?"

"It's just not realistic. If it could be done, someone would have done it already. You have to go way back in to get to where they drop their antlers. Miles and miles. Then you have to get them out. There's no way to do it. Are you going to pack out one or two truckloads on your back at night? Nope."

"How about using horses?"

"I hate horses. And, anyway, too much of a production. You'd need to park a trailer at a trailhead, get backcountry permits. They look hard at horse people in the park. You bring a bale of the wrong kind of hay into the park, they fine your ass. No way. I'm done talking about it. I got a date with a cheeseburger and a hot shower. See you next time."

Thad slid the rifle back behind the seat and got in before the Scot could say anything more. He fired the truck and pulled a U-turn, wheels spinning mud. Hazen waved as they passed the Scot, still standing next to his Suburban, watching them go, the sun burnishing his coppery hair.

Thad didn't breathe easy until he'd put a few turns between himself and the Suburban.

"That guy," Thad said, shaking his head. "Screw loose, I think."

"How about that song she played, huh? That was something."

"Every time I look at him all I can think of is that kid he killed. And then when you've done it once it's like it's not a big deal anymore. Doing it again wouldn't be any major thing."

"Pretty amazing. A girl playing those bagpipes like that. I like that music. Do they put that on CDs? I've never seen a bagpipe CD anywhere, but I'd like to have one."

"You knew that kid, right? I mean he was younger, but still, you knew him? What kind of person does something like that? Right in front of his daughter."

"How young do you think she was when she started playing those bagpipes?" Hazen said. "Probably really young for her to be that good already. I wonder how them things even got invented. Crazy."

Hazen hummed a little bit of "Amazing Grace."

They crossed the river on the Cinnabar bridge, the water low and clear, a gray line on the rocks like a bathtub ring where the water had receded since the early summer snowmelt. Thad slowed going over the bridge, and they craned their necks to see over the railing. He could just make out the dark streamlined shapes of several nice trout finning in a slow eddy formed behind a large midstream boulder. They were stacked together almost as if in formation, brown trout probably, staging before the spawn, a period of time in which the males took on brilliant orange and gold colors and grew more aggressive than usual.

Thad drove the winding river road down the valley. The cottonwoods lining the banks were green-tinged pale yellow.

Within a month the branches would be bare and black, snow in the high country, cold wind sliding down the faces of the mountains, funneling into the valley, ripping through the river corridor. Thad did not relish the thought of impending winter; it always seemed to come too soon, stay too late. The envelope was next to him on the seat, and he put his hand on it to feel the thickness. There was the roof, and the truck would probably need new tires this winter, and their propane tank was near empty. Those were just the basics. There were hospital bills too. Debt, a creature that sometimes seemed to open its mouth to him. A great swallowing maw. He drummed his fingers on the bank envelope while he ran the figures—adding and then subtracting, subtracting, subtracting. That's how it always seemed to go.

THAD HAD TAKEN TO PUTTING A HEAVY LENGTH OF logging chain across their driveway with a "No Trespassing" sign on it whenever they left for more than a day. He wasn't sure what made him do it. They'd never had a break-in. Hardly a solicitor, even. He put up the chain and tried to remember if he'd locked the door, if the coffee maker was off, the furnace set on low. He figured it was all part of some sort of panic that grew out of ownership. The house, the yard, the shed, the thirty acres of river-bottom cottonwoods all seemed to rest upon him, literally—on the paperwork he'd signed for the bank after his father's death, a list of assets piling up above his scrawled signature. But what could a man do but breathe deep, shoulder the burden? If it had weighed on their father, he'd never showed it. Maybe you got used to it, like carrying a heavy pack. Maybe it was something you felt strange without when it was gone.

Thad nosed into the driveway and stopped for Hazen to get out and unhook the chain. The thing was—the chain was down, coiled in the gravel like a crushed snake.

"We put that up when we left, didn't we?" said Thad, surprised.

"Yeah, I did it, I remember."

"Did you lock it?"

"I think. Maybe the wind blew it down."

"You think? The wind? What are you talking about, the wind? That chain weighs fifty pounds."

Thad got out and went to the fence post. He'd wrapped the chain around the six-inch spruce post and then pounded a heavy stainless steel timber framing nail through one of the links, with a washer on the head to hold it in place. The other side he'd wrapped around another post and secured with a padlock. The padlock was still on, but the framing nail had been torn from the post, leaving a splintered hole of raw wood.

Thad got the rifle from behind the seat. He gave the keys to Hazen and climbed into the truck bed, racking a cartridge into the chamber.

"You drive," he said. "Go slow. I'll be back here."

Their driveway was long, their house set back away from the road, right next to the river. Their mother's father had built the house with his own hands. He felled the trees for logs and brought them down from the hills, chained to a two-horse team, skidding them across the snow in midwinter. He stripped them by hand with a drawknife and set the massive rounds in place with nothing but a system of levers, ropes, and pulleys. It was low-ceilinged for this very reason. It wasn't beautiful; it seemed to sprawl across rather than rise up from the ground. But it was easy to heat and the wind blew right over the top of it, and when occasionally the giant sleeping volcano under Yellowstone tossed in its sleep, the house barely let out a creak. Up until he'd taken sick, Thad's father had been religious about maintenance. He'd re-chinked the whole place by himself, at least twice. Rebuilt the river-stone chimney. Varnished the logs every three years and sprayed for carpenter bees every spring. He'd inherited the house from people he'd never known, and he maintained it as if he were just a caretaker and the real owners would be coming back sometime soon.

For Thad, to look at the place now was to face rebuke. From his father, from his relatives he'd never known. In its current state of disrepair the house seemed to be weathering into its environment. The roof was greenish with moss and mold. Chinking cracked and faded. The varnish was scabbed and peeling so that the logs had come to resemble the rough bark of the cottonwoods that flanked the river.

Coming down the drive, Thad had visions of theft, of burglary, of meth-head vandals shitting on the carpet and slashing the sofas, or of one of the various entities to whom he owed money coming to collect. Or worse, the Scot, somehow beating them out of the woods, sitting on their porch with his pistol and a smile. The truck continued to move, and he knelt in the back with the safety off. He couldn't think of a single good thing that could be waiting for them at the end of the drive.

As they rounded the last curve, their house became visible through the trees, and Hazen brought the truck to a halt. There was a dusty brown Econoline van parked in front of the shed. One of its rear tires was shredded so badly it listed, resting on a bent rim. A clothesline ran from a side mirror to a low branch of a nearby cottonwood sapling. On it, clothing flapped in the breeze: pale things, faded T-shirts, bleached cotton underwear, washed-out skirts, articles that looked less like clothing and more like trash, scraps of fabric blown there by the wind.

Hazen let the truck idle and opened his door. Thad stayed where he was. They both watched. The van jostled occasionally, clearly occupied. They could hear music, faintly, coming from inside. It sounded like the Doobie Brothers. "China Grove." A female voice joined in singing, not a bad voice, just several beats behind, as if the song she was following were slower.

Hazen got out and slammed the truck door. The singing in the van stopped, and they could see a pale face pressed to the rear window. The face disappeared, the van door slid open, and she got out. She wore jeans cut off at the knees and sandals and no shirt. She was small, with tangled gray-brown hair that seemed to fight its way down her shoulders, ending raggedly above her sagging, bare breasts.

"Jesus," said Hazen, looking at the ground and grinding the toe of his boot into the gravel.

Thad flicked the safety on the rifle. "Uh," he said, and then cleared his throat loudly.

She turned and pulled a T-shirt from the clothesline. Before she pulled it over her head, Thad could see her back, all the vertebrae protruding, knobby and defined as a starved late-winter mule deer. She turned to face them and shielded her eyes with one hand, looking up at Thad standing in the truck bed.

"What are you doing here?" Thad said, realizing even as he said it that it sounded ridiculous.

She didn't say anything, squinted, and came toward them, her sandaled feet making long scuffing sounds in the gravel. It was as if she were walking through mud and having a hard time getting her feet to move.

"I missed you boys," she said.

HER NAME WAS SACAJAWEA, AND SHE'D BEEN A SPOradic mother. No way a person with a name like that could be normal. That's what Thad thought. She'd come and gone for most of their childhood. It started seasonally. One winter, when the boys were able to look after themselves while their father was at work, she'd driven off in her rusty Tacoma, only showing back up, tanned and happy-seeming, when the snow had melted. She brought presents: an abalone shell for Thad, a shark's tooth for Hazen, a case of wine for their father. She'd worked on a vineyard, and that first night she was back she made them spaghetti and meatballs and let the boys have a half glass of red. Thad had hated wine ever since.

Back then she'd adopted a certain way of talking to them. She'd tell them stories about her childhood as if she were a character and the events of her life were just a book she was reading aloud.

She told them how she'd gotten her name. Her father had been fascinated with the Corps of Discovery and greatly lamented the fact that everything had been mapped and charted by the time he'd appeared on the scene. "They passed right through here," he'd say, "Lewis and Clark, and all the rest. Right through this very valley. At the time it was like going to Mars. They had no idea what was out there. There were no maps; hell, they made the maps."

When she came into the world bawling and kicking and calling out in a thin reedy little whistle, her father had said that she looked helpless as a baby bird, that she was his bird child and, even though her mother had wanted to name her Melissa, her father would not be swayed. "Sacajawea means 'bird woman' in Shoshone," he explained patiently to his wife, holding the baby in the hospital bed. "It's the most beautiful name there ever was."

Thad and Hazen had never met their mother's parents. They'd both died in a car accident when Sacajawea was a teenager. All Thad knew about them was from the stories Sacajawea told. According to her, they were freethinking, resourceful ranchers. Hardworking, but also natural musicians. People who went around all day with a laugh and a song on their lips, people who never took pharmaceutical medication or consumed alcohol, who never raised their voices or had a bad word to say about anyone. From a young age, Thad had figured that things would have been different if his mother had been given a straightforward, decent name, like Melissa. It was a near miss. If his grandmother had gotten her way all those years ago, instead of his grandfather, things would have turned out better for everyone.

Her seasonal comings and goings continued for years, until the boys were in their late teens, and then, one spring, the snow melted, and the river rose, and the cottonwood buds popped, and the sandhill cranes stilted in the wet fields, and Sacajawea never reappeared.

THAD TOLD HER SHE COULD STAY FOR A WEEK. THAT was two weeks ago, and her van was parked in the exact same spot as the day she showed up. It seemed settled there somehow, leaning indolently on the shredded tire.

That first afternoon, after stowing the gear and drinking two fortifying beers, Thad had gone to the van. He pounded on the door. He hadn't showered yet and was aware that he smelled. She opened the door and smiled widely, blinking in the sun. Thad said, "He died last year. If you care to know." He'd wanted to pierce and deflate her. Leave her a wobbling pile of empty skin. He wanted to see all her fluids draining through the van's floorboards, disappearing into the dry suck of moisture-starved ground underneath. Her smile hadn't wavered. It may have even grown incrementally. He turned and walked back to the house.

In the mornings she struck strange poses in the grass next to the driveway. She dipped and bowed; she pressed her palms together in front of her and closed her eyes, breathing deeply. Thad would almost forget she was there and then he'd come out on the front porch with his coffee and there she'd be, back arced, forearms on the ground, her hair in her eyes. She hummed, or maybe chanted, Thad wasn't sure—it was too quiet to make out words—and then she rose, making movements with her arms, her fists clenched as if she were punching in slow motion. When she noticed Thad watching her, she would stop and wave and Thad would shake his head and go back inside. He liked his morning coffee on the porch. Her presence unsettled him, made his coffee bitter, set his day off on a bad trajectory.

And then, this morning, he'd come out and there she was doing her tai chi or whatever it was, and Hazen was by her side, trying his best to copy her moves. Thad stood watching Hazen, who had kicked his boots off, as he pirouetted slowly on one stockinged foot, raising his other leg as if delivering a slow-motion roundhouse kick. He lost his balance, staggered, and nearly fell, laughing, his hair flopping around his face.

Thad's coffee had gone cold and he tossed it off the porch. "Hazen," he yelled, "get your shit. Let's go fishing."

He went inside and filled a thermos with coffee, and when he came back out Hazen was loading waders and rods into the back of the truck and their mother was sitting on the rear bumper of the van, smiling, her arms crossed over her chest like she was cold, watching Hazen.

"Good luck," she said as they loaded up. "Have fun."

Thad ignored her, slammed his door, and pulled out in a spray of gravel.

"I don't want you talking to her," he said.

Hazen was sitting in the passenger seat with his fishing vest on. "I wonder what she's eating," he said. "She's been out there for two weeks. Whatever she had with her must be about run out by now."

"I really don't care," Thad said. "Maybe she'll starve to death. I'm getting sick of seeing that stupid hippy van and having to look at her doing those stupid hippy karate moves in my front lawn every morning."

"Maybe she wants to stay."

"She's not going to stay. She's on borrowed time already. I'm not letting her stay, even if she wants to."

"I wonder where all she's been," Hazen said.

Thad rolled down the window and spit. "I couldn't care less."

They drove in silence. As they neared the river, Hazen riffled through the pockets of his vest and came up smiling. "Check this out." He had a metal fly box and he opened it, revealing a neatly regimented collection of flies, wooly buggers and bitch creeks and Montana nymphs—heavy wet flies, the only kind their father ever used. "These are some of the last ones he ever tied. He gave them to me that last time we took him out fishing. Remember that? Even stuck on the edge of the river in that wheelchair I think he caught more than you."

Hazen removed an olive wooly bugger from the box and held it up, stroking the hackle feathers back, regarding it with one eye squinted slightly. "*Proper proportions provide a pleasing presentation.* Remember him and that ruler? I hated that ruler."

Thad and Hazen had been homeschooled until they were old enough for high school. Their mother had taught them to read. Thad had dim memories of the woodstove throwing its orange flickering glow so the whole inside of their living room pulsed like a warm interior borealis, his mother sitting cross-legged reading from *Where the Wild Things Are*. She'd read it so many times she had it memorized. She held the book up to Thad and rotated it slowly to Hazen and back so they could see the illustrations, the strange creatures shifting and moving in the firelight. Her voice soft. *Please don't go. We'll eat you up. We love you so.* And then, not long after Thad and Hazen could do a passable job reading the book to her, she left. Thad realized that it was probably foolish to tie the two events together in his mind, but he remembered for a long time thinking that if he had continued to stumble over words, if he'd been unable to make order of the sentences, his mother would have never gone.

In her absences their father picked up where she'd left off. He taught them as best he could, emphasizing areas in which he had some level of expertise, glossing over subjects that had never interested him. From him the boys had learned geometry—he'd been a carpenter—and something of geology. He hiked with them up to Two Ocean Pass and they threw sticks in the creek there at the parting of the waters. *That stick is headed to the Pacific*, he said. *And that one is going to the Gulf of Mexico. This creek splits right at the Continental Divide. There's no other place like this in the whole country. Jim Bridger discovered this back in the day, and for a long time no one believed it was true.*

He taught them a version of American history that was slightly skewed from that presented in the history books. He'd read somewhere that the Vikings discovered America and had been living peacefully with the Native Americans for hundreds of years before Columbus staggered ashore. He told them that they were descended from that mix, part Viking, part Iroquois. To them this was better than being told the blood of kings flowed in their veins. They played Vikings and Indians, one brother leading the noble tribe, the other leading a crew of courageous seafarers far from home. The battles in the cottonwood stand next to the river were violent and convoluted; often it wasn't clear if Vikings and the Iroquois were sworn blood enemies or sworn brothers in blood.

Their father kept them tired. If he had a parental philosophy, it was that exhaustion made for good behavior. Daily hikes in the mountains, their short legs working overtime to keep up with his long stride. Sometimes he would outpace them on purpose, leaving them gasping and scrambling up and down slopes, calling for him in panic only to have him circle around and appear behind them laughing. *Be comfortable*, he'd say. *People who are comfortable in their own skin can never get lost.* He'd stand and wave his arms around as if gathering the peaks and ponderosas and the great leaning chunks of sheared-off granite boulders to him. *All of this can be your home if you're comfortable in here.* He'd make his arms move in slowly so it was just his hand encompassing a little circle in the middle of his chest. *Right here is where you control your world.* So, in that way, he saw to their religious education.

He taught them to shoot, to ski, to swim, the basics of small engine repair, the essentials of carpentry, and, of course, how to fish. How to cast a fly rod and wade the big roaring river that changed its face each year with the reshaping force of runoff. In the long winter evenings, after he'd taken them skiing or snowshoeing and worn the edge off their deep reserves of boyish energy, he'd set up the card table in the living room in front of the woodstove and teach them to tie flies, to turn lengths of peacock feather and elk hair and yarn and tinsel into imitations of small fish and insects that would fool the trout into biting. He was meticulous and laid down strict guidelines he expected the boys to follow. The marabou tail on a size-four wooly bugger should be one and a quarter inch long, no more and no less. The thread head should be one eighth of an inch long and perfectly tapered, whip finished and made glossy with head cement, no exceptions. All work was checked with a small ruler, and all flies that didn't pass muster were unceremoniously stripped down to the bare hook with a razor blade. Naturally, the boys hated fly tying. Hazen especially was confounded by their father's unyielding adherence to regulation and on more than one occasion was reduced to tears while trying to correctly wrap a smooth floss body or mount a pair of matched hackle wings on a feather streamer. In the end, though, Hazen had prevailed in his own way. He would wrap great messy gobs of material on large hooks and go out and catch more fish than anyone.

Thad remembered Hazen, maybe twelve years old, holding out a large trout he'd caught for their father's approval. "It's not the fly," Hazen had said, "you just got to get it in the right spot." Even all these years later, Thad could remember his brother's laugh, ecstatic, slightly terrified, the thundering awareness that comes instantly to all boys when they realize for the first time that the way of their father is not always the best way.

Thad sat on a rock and watched Hazen, knee-deep in the river, reel in another trout. It was a nice brown, and Hazen held it aloft, a finger hooked under its gill for Thad to see. Hazen waded ashore and knelt at the edge of the river. He found an egg-sized rock, pinned the thrashing trout to the ground, and dealt it a single sharp blow to the top of the head that made it shiver one long nerve-ridden convulsion and then it was still. Hazen looked up and smiled.

"I'm going to bring this one home for her," he said. He held the trout up again, and when he did a stream of roe poured from its vent, warm orange translucent globes that fell upon the rocks like beads from a broken necklace.

"A female," Hazen said. "That's good. They taste the best."

He pulled out his knife and slit the trout's pale gold belly from throat to anus and with two fingers stripped out the intricate coilings of intestine, laying aside the twin strips of membrane-attached roe, gold and dripping like honeycomb. He took his thumbnail and scraped it along that kidney-colored line running the length of the trout's inner spine and let the current wash and rinse the stuff away until the inside of the trout's cavity was clean and pink. He held it up again for Thad's approval.

"She'll like this one," he said. He laid the trout out on a rock and sat down, and Thad didn't say anything. They both watched the river and then the wind came up just a little and all the cottonwood leaves that had been just barely clinging to their hold on the branches succumbed and flew.

Thad had seen it before in falls past. One day the cottonwoods were fully clad in gold, and the next they were stripped bare, marking the passage of season more clearly than any calendar could show. It was like being shaken up in one of those Christmas snow globes. Whole trees denuded in an instant, like a flock of gilded starlings taking flight, only to devolve into swirling chaos, landing in mats on the river, tumbling in the current, covering Thad and Hazen where they sat on the edge of the river, covering the rocks, covering the dead trout as if out of some nature-born modesty, everything burnished in a light layer of heart-shaped gold leaf.

Hazen had leaves in his hair, covering his legs, resting like fallen petals on his shoulders. He was laughing. And then the sun went briefly behind a small cloud and the light went metallic and it got noticeably colder, and Thad, who had been feeling pretty good, was filled with that aimless dread that always preceded the shortening of days, the coming snow, bared branches, everything dampening down under the knowledge that soon the sun was going to be giving all its attention to another hemisphere.

Thad took the slow route home. He'd opened a beer and had the windows cracked. It wasn't warm enough to roll them down fully, but he liked to smell the crispness, the smell of dying leaves and dried-out grass and the damp of the snow hiding in the clouds, building up over the peaks like the pulse behind the eyes that precedes a migraine headache.

On the high bridge over the river he slowed to a stop and looked upstream into Yankee Jim Canyon. He could hear the subdued roar of the water constricted by the soaring cliff walls. Above this canyon lay another, and another after that, more tortured whitewater and cliff walls and fallen boulders. The canyon names were themselves ominous: Hellroaring, Black, and Grand. The river drained out cold and green from country that few visited and no one called home. Places where the earth's crust was so thin it was like a scab over a molten wound. The air sulfurous, great gouts of steam rising, the very ground pulsing with the Vulcan pressure seething below. Great herds of elk and bison wandered the high plain here, taking shelter in the lee side of sculptured drifts of wind-packed snow, wallowing in the sulfurous mud at the edge of hotpots that at their center took on the otherworldly aquamarine and ocher and carmine hues of the algae that thrived somehow in their superheated cores.

Sometimes an animal would get too close, and a hoof would punch through the roof of the earth and into another world. If the animal was lucky, its thrashing would widen the void and it would plunge in completely, death if not painless then at least quick. The less fortunate would pull themselves out, staggering and bawling through the mud, flesh peeling off in great blistering swaths, and wander away from their kind, where eventually packs of wolves or solitary grizzlies would finally drag them to the ground.

Thad sat in his truck looking upstream to Yellowstone, thinking, and then, as if summoned somehow by the shape and gist of his thoughts, he saw, in his rearview, a black Suburban turning off the river road. He put his truck in gear and hurried off the bridge toward home.

Hazen had saved the bright-orange globules of roe from the trout he'd killed, and Thad sliced some potatoes thin and fried them in butter with onions and then in another pan fried six eggs and the roe, and he and Hazen ate out on the porch, their plates on their knees looking out across the yard toward the van, where she sat cross-legged in the sun, a blanket wrapped around her shoulders, her back against a cottonwood trunk.

"I went to give her the trout," Hazen said, "but she didn't want it. She drinks this juice. That's pretty much all she eats. It's kind of vinegary, and it has stuff floating in it like the egg drop soup from The Wok. She says it has all the nutrients you need to survive. I asked her if she's been out in California this whole time, and she said she was for a while but not lately. I don't know where all she's been. I guess if you had a van like that you could just go anywhere you wanted and then pull up stakes when you got bored with it."

Thad had been leaning back in his chair. He settled it back on all fours with a thump and went in to do the dishes.

HE WOKE TO WATER DRIPPING ON HIS FACE. THERE'D been a dream, but upon waking the dream was immediately gone and whatever insights or glimpses into the unconscious it might have afforded were lost upon him. He didn't put much stock in them anyway. Hazen, on the other hand, could talk for hours, in great, tedious detail, about the events that had transpired when he fell asleep. "There's two worlds," he'd said once. "They sit there like two rooms side-by-side in the same house, and sleep is a door that opens for a while so you can go back and forth." Thad wondered where his brother had come up with that one. He thought it sounded like hippy bullshit, and he'd told Hazen so.

Thad lay on his back in bed—the same one he'd slept on his whole life. Under the same low roof. Every so often a drip would form on one of the exposed log beams above him and would swell and grow until it reached terminal capacity, and then it would fall, hitting him at a point just below his right cheek. The mattress around his face bloomed wet. The same double mattress since he was a child. In the same place, in the same room. Hazen's room was across the hall. His father's at the hall's end, empty now. There was only one world, of that Thad was fairly certain. Sleep had no power to lead you anywhere. A dream was nothing. Not a directive, or evidence of a grand design, certainly not a preview of an afterlife.

It had rained all night. He'd fallen asleep to the sound, and now in the bleak flower of dawn it rained on. Another roof leak to add to the one in the living room, the two in the kitchen. Thad shifted his head from the wet sheets. His father's bed had been wet at the end, too, foul. And when he was finally gone Thad and Hazen had dragged it to the backyard, spilled diesel fuel over it, and set it on fire. On that day Thad had remained beside the mattress for a long time, hands in his pockets, chin tucked down into the collar of his jacket, watching it burn until there was nothing left save the coiled metal springs. They glowed white hot, then orange, fanned by the wind funneling down the river.

Above him in the gloom another drip gathered and formed and Thad lay there, waiting for it. Before waking there'd been a dream, that much he knew. His father coming to him, telling him something. Advice. Solutions. Showing him the way, if only he could remember.

Eventually Thad rose and moved his bed away from the drip. He pulled on his jeans and went to the kitchen for a large metal bowl, the one his father had liked to put his microwave popcorn in, and he positioned it on the floor under the leak. On the way back to the kitchen, to start the coffee, he kicked his brother's door to wake him up.

Coffee and eggs and then work. Dreams didn't have the power to exist in this world, and so they lacked the strength to effect outcomes. A dream solution could only fix a dream problem, and Thad's problems—seemingly increasing in number every day—were of a more tangible kind.

THEY'D BEEN WORKING THE MICROBURST UP MILL Creek for years. An old Forest Service road switchbacked up a steep hill to a long flat ridge where, at some point a decade or so ago, an angry wind had ripped through a dense stand of lodgepole and fir, creating a hundred-acre tract of fractured, leaning, hanging, crisscrossed, jackstrawed timber. God's own game of pickup sticks. Thad had looked it up one time, what exactly causes a microburst. Apparently, it had something to do with air pressure, a down draft in an overhead thunderstorm that produces an extreme outward burst of wind near the surface of the ground. They hit only small areas with hundred-mile-per-hour blasts, or more. They lasted only a few seconds and came completely out of the blue. In this case, what remained was good wood—plenty of it standing or leaning, dried a silver gray—but brutal work. There were sharp stobs of broken-off branches that seemed to clutch and grab at every loose article of clothing. Thad didn't have a single work shirt that hadn't been snagged and ripped at least once. Widow-makers everywhere, the trees laced together in incomprehensible configurations. At one point they had come across two uprooted lodgepoles completely upended and then skewered back down into the ground, tortured roots to the sky. That one had been a head-scratcher. Some upside-down tree species from an alien planet where the role of the sky and the earth had been reversed.

Thad drove slowly, easing their old long-bed Ford around the hairpin corners heading upslope. The rain had stopped and the morning was cool. Hazen was blinking away sleep on the other end of the bench seat. He had a cup of coffee in one hand and was trying to time his sips in between bumps. His jeans were splattered.

"Everything's going to be wet," he said.

"So?"

"We could've waited till tomorrow."

"Then what would we have done with today?"

"Could've fished."

"Our roof is a sieve."

"Doesn't bother me."

"You can't live in a house where the roof leaks."

"Why not?"

"You let things go and let things go and then the roof falls in. That's why not. We're fixing that damn thing before the snow flies, end of story. We got people who want wood, and we need to make money, and so we're going to be doing this for the foreseeable future. That's how it is."

Thad pulled into their cut area and reversed the truck so the bed was closer for loading. Hazen finished his coffee and put his mug on the dash. "There's that other stuff we could do instead."

"I'm not talking about it now. Let's go." Thad got out and dropped the tailgate. He slid the saw out and checked the gas. Hazen was out of the truck now, stomping around. He kicked a lodgepole sapling and it released a silver shower of water droplets.

"It'd be better than doing this," he said. "Every single goddamn thing is wet."

Hazen said something more, but Thad fired up the Stihl and gassed it a few times to drown him out. Thad walked to the edge of where they'd called it quits the last time to start bucking up what he'd already laid down. He looked over his shoulder, and Hazen was putting on his gloves. He was shaking his head. His lips moving. He kicked another lodgepole sapling and then hefted the maul to start splitting rounds.

By the early afternoon, Thad cut his way into a particularly gnarly section of timber, a dozen or more trunks knit together in a dense, conical, leaning configuration—a shape that almost seemed to suggest preordination, a dwelling of some kind, a wickiup wind-crafted by a mad god. There was good wood in there, a lot of it. Thad killed the saw and stood, pondering, trying to figure out an angle of attack that wouldn't result in the whole mess coming down on his head. Eventually he decided to eat a sandwich and think about it.

Hazen had a large pile of split pieces next to the truck. The wood was straight grained and dry and burst eagerly at the head of the ax. Back at the house, they already had a trailer full, split and ready to go. That and a three-quarter load in the bed would be enough for the two deliveries he'd promised. Thad didn't like driving the truck with it loaded all the way down; it squatted considerably and groaned around corners. Hazen had the Igloo out and was sitting on a stump, peanut butter and jelly smeared on his chin. Thad sat on the tailgate and drank from his water bottle, rinsed his mouth out and spit. "Toss me my sandwich," he said.

Without looking at him Hazen reached into the cooler and found the foil-wrapped sandwich. He sidearm-Frisbee tossed it with force, and it sailed wild past Thad, landing in a pile of wet sawdust and cut limbs.

"Hey, asshole," Thad said. "Now get up and bring it to me."

Hazen remained seated, staring straight ahead. He took a large bite of his sandwich and chewed noisily. Thad's water bottle was cylindrical aluminum with a plastic handle on the screw lid. It was half-full, and he hooked two fingers through the handle and threw it end over end. It hit Hazen it the ribs and he slid off the stump, clutching his side, sandwich in the dirt.

Thad hopped off the tailgate, ready for Hazen to push off the ground and come at him, but he didn't. Hazen rolled over so his back was to the stump and reached for what was left of his sandwich. He ate it there silently, sitting in the muddy track he'd made going back and forth loading all morning.

"What?" Thad said. "What's your problem today?"

"This is stupid. We could just go out and look around. I know where we could go. It's easier than this."

"I'm sick of hearing about it. There are consequences. Use your head for once in your life. We can't make that a regular thing. We get caught and then what? We're fucked, that's what. Imagine going to jail. How does that sound?"

"How would we get caught?"

"And besides that, the whole thing is just greasy. It's a waste. That's not how we were raised. Could you imagine what Dad would have thought? Just leaving them to rot like that?"

"What about the other thing then? Is picking up a few sheds really that big of a deal?"

"The Park Service would say yes. Up there, you're not just picking up antlers. You're stealing a national treasure. Trust me, I've thought about it. There's no way to do it right. How many do you think you could carry on your back? Not enough to make it worth our while, I can tell you that."

Hazen shrugged. "I still think we could do it with horses, or mules. Or maybe we could get a four-wheeler or dirt bikes up in there with some kind of little trailer."

"Or why don't we just buy a helicopter and airlift them out? Jesus. I don't want to hear about it anymore."

Thad fetched his sandwich and ate it leaning against the hood of the truck, his back to Hazen. It was a dry affair, sourdough, bacon, and onion. There'd been no mayonnaise left in the jar this morning. Apparently, Hazen had put the jar back in the refrigerator, empty, after the last time he'd made a sandwich.

Thad mechanically chewed and swallowed, chewed and swallowed, watching a pair of chickadees chase each other through the windfall. He threw his crust into the brush and pulled on his gloves. He was thirsty, and when he retrieved his water bottle he found that the top had come off. He drank the last few teaspoons that remained at the bottom and kicked Hazen's boot as he walked by.

"Get your ass up and help me with this."

In the mess of twisted trunks and limbs, Thad isolated a small lodgepole that didn't seem to be bearing any weight and severed its base. With Hazen's help he managed to pull it from its mooring and slide it out onto the flat ground for bucking up. They were able to remove a few more trees this way, and they dragged them next to the first. The trees that remained were larger, locked together in a tight dead embrace of needleless branches.

Thad told Hazen to get back, and he wiped the wet sawdust from his face with his sleeve. He juiced the saw a couple times and started to make a cut on the trunk that seemed to be supporting most of the weight. He held an awkward stance, the saw at arm's length to give him distance in case the trunk decided to splinter under the weight of the other trees leaning into its crown. Halfway through Thad could feel the saw starting to bind, and he backed it out momentarily. He made another push, and at that point the cut opened like a yawning yellow mouth. Thad hopped back and there was a rifle-shot crack as the trunk broke through. The whole mess sagged for a moment and then began a slow topple in the direction where Hazen was standing. He was safely out of range of the tallest tree, standing there, arms crossed, watching it go. When the still-tangled wad of timber crashed to the ground, something happened that Thad couldn't quite see. Hazen let out a pained shriek and went down, hunched over on all fours.

Thad killed the saw and made his way through the log jumble. Hazen was coughing and spitting in a fetal position with his hands clutched between his legs. There was blood on the inside of his thigh, and Thad tried to turn him over to see what had happened but Hazen elbowed him and rolled away, cursing. He managed to sit up and he spread his legs, looking down at himself. He had a gash on the inside of his left thigh. His jeans were torn and there was blood. "Let me see it," Thad said.

"Fuck you."

"What happened? I couldn't see."

Hazen pushed up to his hands and knees and then stood, holding his crotch. From that angle Thad could see that the gash wasn't too bad; it was barely bleeding. It was long, six or seven inches, but not deep. "It doesn't look that bad," Thad said. "Let me see it."

Hazen pushed by him and shuffled toward the truck in a half crouch.

"What the hell even happened? Did something fly off and hit you?"

Hazen didn't say anything until he'd pulled himself into the cab of the truck. He curled up on the front seat.

"We should wash that cut out."

"It's not the cut. I was standing over one of those small logs we pulled out first. Then when you dropped the rest of them, they landed on the other end of it and it came up and racked me in the balls."

"Jesus. Are you OK? Should we look at it?"

"Leave me alone. Shouldn't even have been up here. I've been soaking wet all day."

"You're still on that? I need to know if is this an injury or are you just a little hurt?"

"Leave me alone. I'm done for the day."

Thad left Hazen and went back to the saw. He bucked up the fallen logs and then he started splitting. By midafternoon he'd loaded enough to call it good. Thad secured the saw and the jerrican on top of the cut wood in the back, and they began the slow drive down the mountain. Hazen was sitting normally, head leaned against the passenger-side glass.

"You going to make it?" Thad said eventually.

"I guess. No thanks to you."

"It's not my fault. I'm sorry, but it was an accident. We'll go home and you can get cleaned up. Take a couple Tylenol. Shouldn't take us too long to get these people their wood, and then we knock off for the day. I'll buy you a beer and a burger at the Goose. Deal?"

Hazen pressed his crotch gingerly. He stared ahead for a moment and then he held a hand up in Thad's direction with four fingers splayed.

"What?"

"Not *a* beer. Four beers. I looked at myself. I'm going to have black-and-blue balls. I can already tell. Four beers, or I'm done."

"All right, bud. We'll see."

Thad's hands were still full of tingle from the saw. The truck smelled like cut pine and gas, and his back was tight from swinging the maul. He pulled out onto the pavement and turned up the river road toward home.

"A good honest day's work," he said, reaching over to punch Hazen on the shoulder. "Eh? Could be worse."

"Tell that to my balls. Four beers. You owe me."

THE FIRST DELIVERY WAS TO A NEWER MANUFACTURED home up on the rocky flats off Caledonia Road. A new home but already there was a piece of vinyl siding picked off by the wind. A trampoline sagged on the side of the driveway. Someone had rigged guy wires to the trampoline's aluminum frame and staked it down to keep it from blowing away. A young woman in a stained sweatshirt answered the door. She had a toddler on her hip. Both were blond and owl-eyed, as if just up from a nap.

"Oh," she said. "The wood. He left you a check. Hope that's OK."

"Fine. We'll get it from you when we're done. Want it in the same spot?"

The woman nodded and the toddler started wailing, slow and low at first. It was as if the child was tuning its voice, getting warmed up. Rapidly the screaming reached an earsplitting pitch and she shut the door in Thad's face.

Thad pulled the truck around back and they started to stack the cord against the back wall of the house, next to the small patio they had there. Hazen had changed his jeans and he was moving stiffly. They cross-stacked the end columns and filled in between them, not speaking. They were nearly done when the sliding door to the patio opened and the woman stuck her head out.

"Oh my god," she said. "I'm so sorry. I can't believe I forgot. He said to tell you to put it over by the shed this time. Putting it up next to the house like that is turning the siding a weird color."

Thad was holding the final armload of the cord, nearly ready to deposit it on the neat stack. He looked at her. The toddler was clutching her knee and he could hear the TV in the background. "I'm so sorry," she said. "Could you move it? The water drips off the roof when it rains and it gets the wood wet and then it turns the siding moldy. I was supposed to tell you then I forgot, and he specifically told me this morning to tell you to put it over by the shed. He'll be super pissed when he gets home. I'm so sorry, guys." The toddler made a face like it was gearing up for another round of screeching, and Thad turned on his heel, walked back to the freshly unloaded trailer, and threw in his armload of wood. Hazen was already leaning against the fender, and Thad gestured with his thumb over his shoulder to the stack of wood.

"Come on," he said.

"Seriously?"

It was evening by the time they loaded the wood back into the trailer, drove it around the house to the shed, unloaded and restacked it. The telephone poles lining the road were the only thing up there tall enough to cast a shadow. As Thad drove slowly out of the yard, their long humanoid shapes stretched across the rocky ground. "She gave us an extra ten bucks for having to move it," Thad said.

"Oh boy."

"I know. Something tells me that asshole would probably have come home and beat on her if we'd left the wood where it was. That's the only reason I agreed to it."

Hazen shifted. He had one hand cupped over his crotch. "Or maybe he'd have come home and moved it himself."

"Could be. Just seemed like that woman might have felt the wrath is all. That was the vibe I got."

"I didn't get no vibe."

"You imagine being cooped up in that trailer with that kid? Jesus."

"Her fault."

"How're your balls?"

Hazen raised one middle finger in Thad's direction, and they rode in silence to deliver the final cord in the gathering dark.

OLD LAUREN HAD LIVED WAY BACK IN UP CINNABAR Basin for as long as Thad could remember. Their father had delivered her wood on and off over the years. Thad remembered once going into her small, stuffy kitchen with his father to receive payment for a load. The place stank of cat piss and she'd made cookies. She paid his father with cash she counted out of a mason jar retrieved from behind a row of canned green beans. She gave Thad a cookie. It was still warm, gooey chocolate chips, but when he took a bite, something was off with it; it was salty. Disgustingly so. He'd held it, chocolate melting on his hand, until they made it back to the truck. When he rolled down the window to throw the cookie out, his father had said, "What, don't you want it? Pass it here."

His father took a bite and chewed, and then his eyes widened and he spit into his hand. "What in the holy hell? Couldn't you give a man a warning? That's just wrong. I believe Old Lauren mixed up her sugar and her salt." He rolled down his window and sent the remainder of the cookie flying.

This was almost twenty years ago, and she'd been old then. Thad didn't know how she was still alive, much less living on her own at the near end of a crooked-ass mountain road.

It had been over a year since they'd been up there, but it didn't look like much had changed. Old Lauren's beat-up Chevy with a railroad tie for a rear bumper was parked out front. Three longhorn cattle stood dumbly in the front yard. *Yard* being a term used loosely to denote the rocky, trash-festooned area in front of her house. There was no grass. The cattle were dusty. One of them had something wrong with its hoof; it moved around haltingly on three legs. The cows were contained by a dilapidated fence cobbled together with bits of baling twine, rope, wire, even a section of old Christmas string lights, the bulbs mostly broken. Cats flitted around the sagging porch. What sounded like a pack of hounds barked and wailed inside the house. Hazen got out to open the gate, and Thad pulled through so he could fasten it behind them. By the time he'd pulled around to the small lean-to off the kitchen where she kept her wood, Lauren was out on the porch. She had a cane now. She wore the same patched pair of Carhartt overalls she always wore. Her hair was long and white and tied back in a ponytail. Cats rubbed themselves against her shins. She thumped her cane on the porch boards to get Thad's attention. "You all shut the gate behind you?" Her voice was deep. Not frail or wobbly like one might expect from someone of her age. She had a man's voice; that's what Thad always thought.

If you weren't looking right at her, you'd never believe that voice was coming out of that little old lady.

"Hi, Lauren. We shut it," Thad said.

"Those steers will slip out on you if you give them half a chance."

"We'll make sure they don't get out."

"And don't get too far along with that wood. Sorry you came all the way up here, but I can't take none of it from you today."

"But you called last week."

"I know I called. Can't pay you. One of my dogs got in a fight with something, raccoon maybe, got all tore up, and I had to take him to the vet. Now I'm broke till next month. If it's not one thing it's another." Lauren bent to rub one of the cats behind its ears. The cat leaned in, eyes closed. "You all are set on keeping me in the poorhouse, aren't you?" she said.

"Think you'll be able to pay us next month?"

"Who knows what could happen next month? I stopped buying green bananas at the County Market a long time ago."

One of the steers let loose a prodigious bellow and then released an equally prodigious stream of shit. The wet sound of its falling filled the yard.

"We came all the way up here," Thad said. He looked down, kicked a rock. "*Farmer's Almanac* is predicting a bad one this year. You're going to need some wood."

"I'm not a charity case yet." Lauren thumped her cane on the porch boards again and the cats scattered.

"Nothing charitable about it. You're a longtime customer. I'm not driving all the way back down the hill with that load of wood. We're going to unload it. Get me back if and when you can. Not a big deal."

"I heard about your father. A shame. He probably did as good a job as he could with you two." Lauren thumped her cane on the porch one more time. She was staring past Thad toward where Hazen was sitting in the cab of the truck.

"Is that your brother in there?"

"Yeah, that's Hazen."

"I watched you two once when you were boys. You remember that? You were pretty young. Your father had to go somewhere. I can't remember where. It was a long time ago." Lauren pointed the rubber tip of her cane at Thad and then angled it to point at Hazen. "I thought he was a strange boy. Every night you cried for your mother. That one never did, though. And he was always watching me. Turn a corner and there he'd be. Big eyes. I was going to cook you boys burgers and I left the bowl of meat on the counter, and when I came back in he'd gotten a chair and was up there with a little handful of bloody meat, eating it. Smeared all over his face. It's a miracle he didn't get sick all over the place."

In the truck Hazen waved.

Lauren brought her cane down with one final thump, turned, and shuffled back inside. Before shutting the door she leaned out. "I'll make you boys a dinner one of these days. I've got a big ol' tom turkey that's been coming in the yard every day. I'll roast him and invite you boys up. I'll have mashed potatoes too."

"All right, Lauren. We're going to get this unloaded before it's pitch-black."

They stacked the last few armloads after the sun had long set. No lights had come on in Lauren's house. Thad wondered if a person of that age slept a lot, or never had to sleep at all. For some reason Thad didn't think she was asleep. He thought she might be just sitting there, in the dark, with her cats, her dogs, her memories. At her age the balance must shift, the weight of memory gathering mass until each waking day was more of a waking dream haunted by the shades of people you'd known who were a long time gone.

On the way down the drive, the truck headlights made legendary beasts out of Lauren's steers. Massive necks and ponderous sweeps of horn. Red-eyed, dust swirling under hoof. Aurochs. Creatures drawn by the fingers of ancestral humans deep in the earth's bowels.

They hit the pavement before either of them spoke. Hazen crossed his arms over his chest. "I knew she wasn't going to have any money."

"Sometimes she does, sometimes she doesn't. Dad always gave her the wood either way, and that's what we'll do too."

"There's no point in it. Everything we did today, for what? Should've just gone fishing."

"Do you remember her coming to watch us for a while when we were kids? She said she did."

"She babysat us?"

"Apparently. Dad had to go somewhere and he called her to watch us."

"And so he gave her wood for free after that?"

"I don't know. Maybe that was part of it."

"I'm not going up there to eat her old yard turkey. Count me out."

"I doubt that will happen. It was just something she had to do, a gesture. We gave her wood, and she gave us the offer of a turkey dinner."

"Why in the hell does she even have those longhorn cows?"

"They're something to have, I guess. Who knows?"

By the time they got home it was too late to head into town for dinner at the Goose. Thad ended up frying elk burgers in the bacon grease leftover in the cast iron from breakfast. They stood in the kitchen drinking beer while the burgers popped and smoked in the pan. Hazen boiled water for the macaroni and cheese looking out the window at Sacajawea's van. "Going to be getting too cold out there for her pretty soon," he said.

"Good," Thad said. "Maybe she'll head south with the rest of the odd ducks."

They ate at the small cluttered kitchen table. Hazen doused his burger with ketchup, his macaroni with hot sauce.

As soon as Thad chewed his first bite, he felt the tiredness creep up on him like a fog. He chewed with no heart and washed the meat down with beer. Lifting the fork required concentrated effort. Nothing like a full day's work for half a day's pay to induce marrow-deep fatigue. Doing it all over again tomorrow seemed impossible. The fact that his father had logged for thirty years was incomprehensible. Thad thought that maybe the men of his father's generation were made of stronger stuff. That was entirely possible. Or maybe it was simply that his father had never come across another option. He'd had to raise two boys, and that was his lot in life. How many times had their father sat at the kitchen table like this after working all day? How many days worse than this had he endured? He'd never warned Thad that this was how it could be. That over the course of a man's life there would be days that made the dawning of the next seem like some kind of punishment, or perverse reward, for simply surviving the last.

Both of them ate hunched over the table without speaking, the sound of their forks hitting their plates loud in the room. When Hazen drained his fourth beer in quick succession, Thad told him that was enough. Eventually Thad pushed his plate away and leaned back. "Maybe we'll fish tomorrow morning," he said. "Let you heal up a little."

Hazen was wiping up the last of his ketchup with the remainder of his hamburger bun. He looked up and smiled. "Yeah? Cool." Hazen slapped his hands on the table and got to his feet stiffly to deposit their plates in the sink. He went to the freezer and rifled around. He pulled out a package of butcher paper–wrapped meat. "Steak sound good for tomorrow?" he said.

"Fine with me."

"OK then, I'm going to bed." Hazen headed to his room carrying the frozen package of venison, and Thad spoke to his receding form. "I'm not eating those steaks after they've been on your balls. I know what you're doing with those. Jesus Christ."

Thad didn't have it in him to do the few dinner dishes. He left the grease-coated pan coagulating on the stove and collapsed into the recliner. They couldn't keep going this way; that was becoming very clear. They needed to do something to get ahead. His father wouldn't have abided a leaking roof. Judgment from the grave can work on a man—Thad was learning that more and more. His father wouldn't have abided illegality either. These two truths were hard to balance. A few guys he knew had started right out of high school at the Stillwater Mine and by now they were making seventy thousand a year. Maybe he should have gone that route. But he couldn't imagine spending a whole workday underground. Something would come up. They just needed a little breathing room.

He ended up falling asleep with his boots on in the recliner, watching a mildly interesting documentary on PBS, one of the five channels they got on their TV. The show was about the history of logging in the Pacific Northwest. Lots of black-and-white photos of bearded men standing beside colossal stumps, crosscut saws slung over their shoulders. Before modern logging equipment, companies would drag the logs into the rivers and float them out to the coast. There were grainy photos of men wearing spiked boots holding long poles, balancing on floating redwood trunks. These men, whose dangerous job it was to guide the logs downstream and break up jams, were called river pigs.

Thad woke in the middle of the night with a start; the beer he'd been holding had spilled down his leg. The TV was still on, an infomercial hawking elasticized shaping undergarments for women. He'd been having a dream in which he shared a redwood log with a small, hairless, pink barnyard pig. Together they were floating serenely downstream, toward a distant ocean.

IT WAS THE HARDEST WINTER ANYONE IN THE VALLEY could remember having endured for thirty or forty years at least. The woodstove alone wasn't enough to keep the pipes from freezing, and so Thad had been forced to run the furnace. They'd burned through a full five hundred–gallon propane tank before March. They hadn't gotten new shingles on the house before the snow hit. Thad listened to the sound of water dripping into stockpots in the living room where the woodstove warmed the roof. The steady plink-plink-plink was an embarrassment.

Thad had continued to ignore Sacajawea as best as he could. She'd somehow moved from her van into their father's bedroom without ever actually getting Thad's consent. There was no mattress in there, and Thad had to assume she was sleeping on the floor. She rarely ate meals with them, and he'd frequently wake up in the middle of the night to the sounds of her boiling water in the kitchen. He didn't know for sure what she did to fill up her hours. Sometimes her door would stay closed all day. Sometimes, when the weather broke, she would sit on a folded tarp in the snow-covered yard all afternoon. Hazen said he saw two male cardinals land on her, one on each shoulder. He said she didn't move a muscle, and that one of the birds leaned in close so that its beak was near her ear, and it stayed that way for a long moment, as if it were passing on a secret to her. Thad told him he was full of shit. "I don't even remember the last time I saw a cardinal," he said.

"Exactly," said Hazen.

Once, when he was loading the woodstove in the living room, he felt her presence behind him and turned and found her standing with her arms crossed over her chest looking at him.

"I always thought that if something happened to him, or one of you boys, I would feel it somehow, no matter where I was. But I didn't. I don't expect you to understand or forgive me."

Thad didn't look at her, spoke to some point over her shoulder. "Don't think you'll ever get a piece of the house or the land. He signed it all over to me. Got your name taken off the deed before he died. I don't care if it was your folks' to begin with; it'll never be yours." He knew this was a petty thing to say. But he had nothing else.

"That's not why I'm here."

"Why then? I don't think you've been real clear on that."

Sacajawea shrugged. "We're born in one spot and spend the rest of our lives trying to get back there."

"That doesn't even make sense."

"It will."

At this point he had stormed off to the shed and left her standing there. This was a month ago, and he hadn't sustained more than two full sentences of conversation with her since. Still, her presence was everywhere in the house. She left used teabags on spoons on the kitchen counters. Strands of her gray hair stuck to the back of the couch. These things enraged him. The fact that he'd almost gotten used to these things enraged him more.

Her van remained in the same exact spot she'd parked it. It sat squat and brown, now resting fully on all four rims, like a hunkering, manure-encrusted rhino.

IT WAS COLD THE DAY THE SCOT CAME CALLING. COLD but clear, a sharp wind coming down the valley from the north. Thad, mostly out of boredom, was on the roof with a tape measure and a notebook, calculating, with some dismay, the number of shingles he would eventually have to purchase. From his vantage point he saw the black Suburban coming from a long way off. Hazen had left earlier that morning on his snowshoes, and Thad had no idea where he was going or when he'd be back. Sacajawea, as far as he knew, was still in her room in some sort of meditative trance. He hadn't seen her in two days. Thad thought about scrambling down the ladder and getting a gun but decided against it at the last minute and sat with his legs dangling off the edge of the roof, snapping the tape measure open and closed until the Scot pulled up.

The Scot made no move to get out of the Suburban. He rolled the window down and gave a strange little wave, the slow wrist rotation of a beauty queen riding a parade float. Thad could see that the girl was in the passenger seat, stocking cap with braids protruding, squinting up at him. The Scot stopped waving and motioned for him to come down. Thad hesitated and then clipped the tape to his belt and descended the ladder, jumping the last few rungs to the ground.

"Home improvements?" the Scot said, gesturing to the roof and the ladder.

"Have a few leaks. Been meaning to get to it, but it seems like it's one thing after another."

"Isn't that the way of it with homeownership? I never knew your father. But I've heard of his passing, and I don't think I ever properly expressed my condolences. I'd like to do that at this time."

"Is that why you came down here?"

"Well, sure, in part. I was just driving by and I thought I'd keep the longstanding rural tradition of unplanned visits alive and well. How's that brother of yours?"

"He's fine."

"You must get tired of having to keep an eye on him all the time."

"I don't have to do too much. Nothing wrong with Hazen."

"No, I guess not."

"Is there something I can do for you?"

"Well, not really. Just consider this a checking-in kind of visit. You remember what we talked about this fall?"

"I remember."

"Wintertime is hard on the pocketbook. I can only imagine what sort of financial situation you must be in after your father's illness."

"None of your concern."

"I'm just saying that if you were to change your mind about doing that thing, I would be very interested in opening dialogue with you in an attempt to get it done in the most mutually lucrative way possible."

"I already decided about that."

"OK." The Scot thumped his heavy fingers on the steering wheel a few times and nodded, making a small clicking noise with his tongue on his teeth. "In the spirit of full disclosure, I feel like I should let you know that I will be contacting your brother to extend him an offer."

Thad put a hand on the partially rolled-down window and leaned in closer. He tried to make his voice as calm and level as possible. "You will do no such thing."

"I beg your pardon?"

"I said, stay away from Hazen."

"I don't see what the problem is. If I'm not mistaken, he's the one with the saleable knowledge in this endeavor. He is the one that knows where the things are. Honestly, I'd put your role here as that of a handler, a middleman, a manager at best, nothing more. I like to cut out the middleman whenever possible. That's just a principle of sound business, if you ask me."

"If you think he could do something like that on his own, you're crazy. You've talked to him. You know."

"What do you mean? You said yourself that there isn't anything wrong with him."

"There isn't. Planning and follow-through just aren't his strong points."

"Well, he wouldn't exactly be wandering alone in the wilderness with no direction. I'd be the guiding hand out there, so to speak."

"He's been known to bite the hand that guides him."

"I highly doubt he'd be foolish enough to bite mine."

"Foolish has nothing to do with it. He just doesn't spend much time thinking about repercussions."

"I'm sure we'd be able to come to a working arrangement. Over the years I've shown myself to be a successful motivator of people."

"We can just stop this conversation now as far as I'm concerned. Hazen won't take a job without me, and I've told you my decision. There's no way to do it safely, end of story."

"What if I told you I'd already talked to Hazen? And that he thinks, with horses, at night, it would be doable?"

Thad had started to turn to walk away but he stopped. He wiped at his running nose and spit into the snow at his feet.

"I've noticed a strange thing in those who serve as caretakers," the Scot said. "They tend to underestimate the abilities of their charges. The more someone needs your care, the more important your own existence becomes."

"What are you trying to say?"

"I'm saying that I think you'd be uncomfortable if your brother didn't rely on you. If your brother set off on his own, Thad, what would you do with yourself?"

"Hazen is free to do whatever he wants. And I know you haven't talked to him, because he hates horses more than I do. Now I got work to do. Take it easy."

Thad turned and walked to the house, not realizing he'd been clenching his fists until he was inside and the door was shut behind him and he could feel his fingernails biting into his palms. There was a little coffee left in the maker, and he poured himself a cup, standing at the window, watching the Suburban recede down the driveway. He took a drink of the coffee. It was burnt from sitting too long on the warmer, and he spit it out in the sink. He knew what angle the Scot was trying to work; it was clear as day.

The way he saw it, there were three possible ways this could go. He could say to hell with it and let Hazen go ahead and make a mess out of everything. He could just roll up his sleeves and try to do the thing as carefully as he could. The final, least likely, but nonetheless problematic possibility was that Hazen, with the Scot's guiding hand, might pull it off without him. The fact that this last outcome troubled him as much as the other two combined seemed to illustrate some finer point of the Scot's bullshit argument. Thad washed out his coffee mug at the sink with such force he broke off the handle.

DURING HIS FATHER'S ILLNESS, THAD HAD GROWN TO hate the mailbox. After one particularly bad mail day, he took the Stihl for a walk down the driveway and cut the treated four-by-four base flush to the ground. He picked up the box and post and heaved it into the brush on the other side of the road.

As it turned out, the state made no allowances for bereavement. The beast of grief might eat everything in its path, but it couldn't digest tax bills, hospital bills, power bills. He could topple the mailbox, delay the inevitable, but in the end the bills still sniffed him out, the broke-stink on him like rot.

When the man Thad's father had used to file his taxes and handle the will finally called, Thad felt something like relief, albeit the bitter relief of the fugitive finally receiving the shackles long-ago made for him.

"I'm doing this as a favor, Thad. I don't want anything from you. Here's the deal—early on, if you'd have dealt with it, we could have gotten a grace period. You should have come to me. Things happen, and there are ways to delay. But you need to be proactive. There's paperwork. And now we've reached this point. This is where we're at. Do you know what a tax lien is?"

It was incomprehensible to him. The hospital bills were astronomical, but they didn't even seem real in a way. No one could pay that much, and Thad had the general understanding that a person could file bankruptcy. It was something he was going to look into, eventually. You can't get blood from a turnip. But this thing was different. The property taxes had been behind for a long time now, and, at some point, an unnamed person or entity had started paying them.

"Why would someone pay my taxes?" Thad said.

There was a pause. "Basically, if you can't make this right, clear up all the back taxes by August 15, the person or persons who've been paying your taxes can take ownership. I mean, technically it goes to the state, but then the state has a tax lien sale, and the person who's invested gets priority. The long and short of it is that you need to take care of this or there's a real chance you lose the house. How did it get this far? I mean, this isn't exactly a fast-moving process. They must've sent you a million notices."

"Who is this person? Do I know them?"

"Thad, they list these things in the paper. By law they have to do it that way, and there's people who use this law as a way to get deals. It's a means of investing. It's not personal. Probably they've been paying the taxes on multiple properties. It could be a corporation. It's a numbers game."

"There's nothing I can do? Can't I get an extension?"

"What you can do is pay the full amount by August 15. At this point there's no wiggle room. You let it go too far. It's the law, and it's cut-and-dried."

"How much?"

When the man told him, Thad didn't say anything. There was nothing to say. He hung up.

TWICE WHILE LEAVING THE HOUSE OVER THE NEXT week, Thad and Hazen passed the Scot parked off to the side of the road near the end of their driveway. Both times he gave them his beauty queen wave as they drove by. In town one day, Thad came out of the hardware store as the black Suburban pulled up next to their truck. Hazen had the window down, and the Scot was leaning over the girl in the passenger seat to talk to him. The Scot was stopped in the road and cars were starting to pile up behind him, honking. He ignored them and then looked up to see Thad coming down the sidewalk. He waved and pulled away.

Thad got in the truck and drove. He didn't say anything. Hazen was quiet until they were almost home, and then he broke.

"He wasn't saying much. Just asking how things were going. Asked me if I had my own truck or if I had to share this one with you. Don't know why he cared really, but I think he was just making talk. Maybe he has one he wants to sell."

"That could be it. Do you want your own truck?"

"Sometimes it might be nice."

"You realize it's not just as simple as that, right? You have to register it. Insure it. Get it licensed. There's forms and fees. All that costs money, and then there's upkeep."

"I know. I don't really need one. I was just talking. The places I like to go mostly you can't get there in a truck anyway."

Thad looked at Hazen out of the corner of this eye. He had the .22 casing in his mouth. He clamped it in one side and then rolled it with his lips and tongue to the other side. Thad could hear it clicking across his teeth.

THE WARM CHINOOK WINDS CAME UP FROM THE southeast and filled the valley with the smell of rotting snow. The river shed its layers of shelf ice and seemed to come awake, readying itself for the great annual runoff. In more temperate locales, this was springtime: daffodils would be raising their leonine heads, grass would be green, people would be sitting outside in the mornings with their coffee, wondering how long they could go before they would need to fire up the lawn mower. Here, in March, there was still six feet of snow in the Beartooths. Down in the valley it wasn't spring; it was mud season. Their driveway froze every night into hard, frost-rimmed ruts but by noon was greasy and soft as melted chocolate. A tedious season. There was very little to do. It was too dangerous to be in the mountains. The strengthening sun touching the face of exposed slopes loosened the snowpack, and the footfalls of a man tromping across it could be enough to shear off a massive slide as thick as wet cement.

It would have been a perfect time to put new shingles on the roof, but of course there was no money for it, and when it came down to it, what was the use of fixing a roof if you stood to lose the house itself? Thad hadn't told Hazen about the call with the accountant. There was no point. Not for the first time, Thad wished his brother was a different way. Someone he could talk with. Formulate a plan with. August 15 was just far enough away that it didn't seem completely real.

Thad came up with housekeeping chores, ones that didn't require spending any money, mostly to keep Hazen in sight.

They replaced the brake pads on the truck and changed the oil and the air filter. They pulled all the gear out of the shed—the axes, the shovels, the tire chains, the snowshoes, the fishing rods and waders and external frame packs and tarps and tents—and piled it all in the wet yard, swept the empty shed, and then put the stuff back in a nominally more organized fashion. When Thad stood and regarded their progress, he was slightly dismayed to see that for all their efforts the shed looked nearly as disheveled as before.

It was too sloppy to get out into the low hills for firewood, but a couple dead cottonwoods had toppled behind the house during the winter storms and they spent several days bucking up the trees and hauling the sections into the backyard to be split. They spent two whole days doing nothing but swinging eight-pound mauls to break the large cottonwood chunks into stove-sized pieces. One of the trees had been huge, much bigger than either of them could reach around with their arms. The twenty-nine-inch bar on the big Stihl chainsaw only made it about halfway through, so Thad had to start the cut first on one side and then finish it from the other. It was a dense, gnarled old tree, especially for a cottonwood, which tended to get soft and punky with age. The rounds from the trunk were too heavy for them to lift, so they had to roll them all the way to the backyard. The first time Thad tried to split one of these big pieces, he swung the maul as hard as he could, and even though he struck dead center in the heartwood, the head only sank about an inch and the round remained perfectly solid, not even a hint of a split. He got Hazen's maul and used the sledge end to drive his own maul deeper into the wood. He pounded until his maul head was completely buried in the wood, and still the wood wouldn't split. He sent Hazen to the shed for their wedges, and finally, when he'd pounded two more wedges into the top of the piece, it split with a groan and pop.

"Jesus Christ," Hazen said. "Look at the grain on that thing. Crookeder than a politician's back." It was something their father had always said. Thad stood up straight, stretched, and leaned against his ax handle. There were moldering piles of dirty snow lingering in all the shadow places between the trees. The air smelled of the burning gas-and-oil mix from the saw and the fresh acrid tang of cut cottonwood. It was as close as anything to what spring should smell like, and for some reason he had to spend a small moment reconciling himself to the knowledge that this year would pass like the last. His father would remain just as dead. Someone had told him that it took the passing of two sets of seasons for grief to subside. He didn't think that was true, but there were times, situations, smells, particular turns of phases that cause the mind to jolt itself awake, and then in that instant, the grief was as fresh as it had ever been.

He breathed deep and spit into the sawdust. "I believe that next one has your name on it, brother," he said.

It took them the rest of the day to split the trunk pieces, and by the time they were done their backs were screaming, their hands raw despite their deerskin gloves. The next day they stacked the mountain of split wood into neat piles at the back of the house, and when it was done they drank a beer sitting on stumps, looking at what they'd accomplished.

"Well, that's done," Hazen said.

Thad finished his beer and turned to look back out over the river. Now that the wood was stacked, he couldn't think of anything to do around the house to keep them occupied. He'd been half expecting another visit from the Scot, and for days now he'd been on edge. Maybe taking off for a while would be a good idea. The Forest Service roads were still too soupy for the truck, but they could walk. A long walk might spur something. A plan. A course of action. "I'm getting bored," Thad said. "We should get out of here and camp for a night or two somewhere. Get a deer, maybe. We just about ate through the jerky from this fall. Maybe we'll poke around a little, glass the hills for bear sign."

"Too early for that, I guess."

"Maybe, maybe not."

"No, I'm pretty sure. It don't smell right yet."

"Smell right?"

"Yeah. I've never seen a bear before I smell a certain smell out there."

"Like what?"

"I don't know. It's close to how its smells now but a little fresher. Right now it's got that kind of smelly moldy-grass-clipping smell and snow and all that. When the bears come out, it smells more like pine. The trees release a smell when the sap starts flowing or something."

"You are so full of shit."

"I'm telling you. The bears aren't out yet."

"So you don't want to go?"

"I didn't say that."

THE AFTERNOON BEFORE THEY WERE GOING TO TAKE off on their camping trip, Thad went to gas up the truck and to get a beer at the Goose. After his beer, he took the back way home. When he hit the raised concrete lip of the cattleguard on Old Yellowstone Trail, he heard something crack in the front end. There was an immediate grinding, and the truck shuddered violently as he braked to a stop in the middle of the road. The cab leaned strangely, and when he got out, he found the front passenger wheel canted at an extreme angle. There was a ragged drag mark on the gravel where the axle had scraped. Thad was fairly certain it was a ball joint or a tie rod, or both. He'd been noticing a slight crunching sound there for a while, but the truck was damn near thirty years old, and if he worried about every squeak he'd never get anywhere. This was not something he could fix himself. This was a tow, a shop bill. A thousand dollars at least, and until it was fixed they had no way to earn a cent. Thad kicked the bumper once and crouched on his heels at the edge of the road. He flipped open his phone and called a tow truck.

After loading the truck on the flatbed, the driver of the wrecker offered to give Thad a ride home. When they pulled up to the house, the Scot's Suburban was parked next to Sacajawea's van. The Scot was standing on the front porch with Hazen. They were both eating apples, looking at Thad.

Thad paid the driver with one of the last hundred-dollar bills he had to his name. As he walked to the porch, he passed the girl, sitting in the Suburban. She watched him go by but didn't acknowledge him. He stopped at the foot of the stairs. The Scot smiled and reached in his coat pocket and threw Thad an apple. Thad caught it reflexively. It was softball-sized, mottled yellow-red.

The Scot pointed to the tow truck receding down the drive. "That didn't look good. Ball joint?"

"Probably.

"You must've been going slow. You're lucky. You'd have rolled if you were on the highway. I've seen it. Not pretty."

Thad looked at the apple he was holding. He contemplated throwing it over the roof of the house toward the river.

"These new apple varieties they're coming up with are remarkable," the Scot said. "That's a Honeycrisp. You ever had one of those?"

Thad shook his head.

"Take a bite. You'll find it just slightly tart. But extremely juicy and firm. That's the most important quality in an apple in my opinion. Firmness. The snap when you bite into it. I can't abide a soft, mealy apple. Try it."

"It's good," Hazen said. He was chewing, and pieces of white apple pulp flew from his mouth.

Thad turned the apple in his hands. "Fine," he said. "We'll do it."

The Scot reached over and slapped Hazen on the shoulder and gave him a wink. "See," he said, "I knew he'd come around to the side of good sense. We'll talk soon." He brushed passed Thad on his way down the stairs, and Thad could smell the tang of the apple on him, along with something sharper, like gun oil.

"One more thing," he said, opening the Suburban door. "Darling, please hand me that envelope in the glove box."

Thad refused the envelope until eventually the Scot grabbed Thad's wrist and placed the envelope in his palm and shook his hand around it, the paper crinkling between their fingers. He smiled as if everything was settled. "You're going to need that truck up and running. Take this as an advance made in good faith. We'll be in touch." The Scot gave Thad a pat on his back and finally released his hand. He ducked into the Suburban, and Thad heard him speak to his daughter. "I was thinking about ice cream. Something about a cold day makes me crave it. Sound good? OK then. To the Dippy Whip we go."

THE SCOT'S CABIN WAS BACK UP IN THE LOW HILLS AT the foot of the mountains. The driveway was long and unmarked except for a "No Trespassing" sign. From the looks of it, the Scot had built the cabin himself. The main building was an A-frame with a stacked stone chimney rising from the tall, peaked roof. There were smaller, low-roofed wings protruding from three sides of the A-frame, and the foundations of these additions were on different levels so that the whole structure looked as if it were somehow emerging from the contours of the land instead of having been constructed on a level plane. The house had a front porch with a railing and columns made of twisted, branching, unprocessed tree sections, the bark still on. The railings dipped and forked, and the columns had hacked-off protruding branches from which hung all manner of things. There was a rusted oil lantern, an empty wooden bird feeder, a metal wagon wheel with spikes upon which dried corncobs had been impaled. There was a magpie-pocked elk hide, flesh side out, stiff and hard as a board. A long silk scarf that had once been red but which had faded to a faint pink in the sun snapped in the wind, its end unraveling. There was a dull white buffalo skull hung from a branch by one ragged empty eye socket. There was a tin bucket with a bullet hole dead center in its middle. There was a crude wind chime made from sun-bleached chunks of antler and bone. The noise it made was hollow and dull, the queasy, unnatural music of bone against bone. On the porch was also a small table, and in its center was a vase containing a decorative arrangement of sorts. Long, dried grasses, branches of red holly berries, a spray of cock pheasant tail feathers.

Thad honked the horn, and then he and Hazen got out and stood in the weak warmth of the early morning sun. It was silent except for the wind in the pines, the occasional clunk of the wind chime. They waited for several long moments for the Scot to emerge. Thad spit and wondered if he should have brought the rifle. The curtains moved across a small window off to the side of the house, and still the Scot didn't show himself.

"Maybe we should knock," Hazen said.

"He knows we're here. I honked the damn horn. I'm not knocking. You knock if you want to so bad." Hazen looked at the porch, the strange gathering of objects hanging there.

"I'm in no hurry," he said. "We can just wait. You ever been up here before?"

"Why would I have ever come up here? The guy has been known to shoot people that come up here."

"Strange house."

"Goddamn weird. The whole thing looks crooked."

"Way back up in here too. I wonder how he gets in and out in the winter."

"Snow machine probably."

"I can't believe he wears that kilt all winter long. Seems like it might get a bit drafty."

"I wouldn't be surprised if he isn't even Scottish."

"Why would he dress up like that if he wasn't?"

"I don't know."

"Why are we here? We've never come up here before."

"Where the hell is he? Clap your hands or something."

"You said yourself, you honked the horn. He knows we're here."

"Fine then. Let's just wait."

Thad sat down on the fender and Hazen hunkered down on his heels, squinting at the house, pulling up tufts of grass. They stayed this way until the soaring skirl of the bagpipes reverberating off the rocky slopes that rose above the cabin brought them to their feet. On a low hillside to the rear of the house, they could see the Scot, tall even at a distance, standing erect with his pipes bristling over his shoulder, his kilt a brilliant red splotch against the pale green of the new grass, the sun glancing off the chrome pistol strapped to his side.

The Scot approached them slowly. As he drew near, the sound of his pipes grew louder until he was pacing back and forth between them, his fingers moving rapidly, his cheeks swollen with air, his eyes clenched into slits, the pipes erupting in deafening blasts. Eventually, after whatever tune he was playing reached a crescendo, he stopped pacing and let the pipes trail off in a low buzz. The sound echoed one final time, and then it was quiet except for Hazen, clapping.

"Boys," the Scot said. "Afternoon." He smiled at Hazen. "This one likes the pipes. Here, take hold of them." He slung the bagpipes off his shoulder and handed them to Hazen, who laughed and stood holding them as awkwardly as a young father who has just been given his firstborn.

"I made the bag myself out of elk hide. The drones are carved bog oak, probably one hundred years old. It's a fine instrument. Not one for the faint of heart. Anyone can play the guitar or the piano or trumpet, but the great highland pipes are a man's instrument. Give it a try."

Hazen shrugged and tried to hand the pipes back.

"No, I mean it. Give the thing a blow. Fill the bag and then put your fingers on the holes there. Squeeze the bag with your elbow."

Hazen, red-faced with effort, managed to get the pipes to emit a single mournful note, somewhere between a cow bawl and a pig squeal, before he dissolved into laughter.

"How'd that make you feel? Feels good, doesn't it? They say that the sound of a bagpipe is enough to make men forget their fear of death. What do you think?"

Hazen looked at Thad and shrugged.

"We've got some stuff to get to this afternoon," Thad said. "So maybe we should just get down to it?"

"All business, this one," the Scott said. He went to the porch and put the bagpipes away in a wooden box on the table. Thad and Hazen sat on chairs rough-hewn from sections of pine log. When the Scot opened the front door, his daughter was standing there as if awaiting direction.

"Coffee, please, darling. And bring some of those scones, thank you." The Scot leaned back into his chair and adjusted his tall wool socks and smoothed his kilt down over the tops of his legs.

"I brought my pipes with me to Vietnam. Humidity was hell on them. I had black mold growing in the bag. Had to stuff newspapers in there overnight. My reeds kept getting waterlogged. In the morning there'd be birds, a whole shrieking demon symphony of them, birdcalls and monkey screeching, the gooks out there yowling with them for all we knew. When it got to be too much, I'd tune myself up. I'd play "Scotland the Brave" as hard and perfect as I could. When I finished, everything would be quiet for a little while. Not a damn sound."

The Scot's daughter came with three cups of coffee on a tray with a small pitcher of cream and a bowl of sugar. She then brought a plate of scones. When she went to go back inside, the Scot motioned for her to sit next to him. "Help yourself, boys. Currant scones, my grandmother's recipe. From the old country. My daughter here is turning into an above-average baker. I hope you don't mind her sitting in on our discussion. It's good to have the female presence in our lives. It's what keeps us from backsliding, reverting back to dark and barbarous modes of behavior."

The coffee was thick and dark, and Thad sipped with his back to the wall of the house. The porch supports with the strange miscellanea hanging from their branches and the twisted, pieced-together bark-covered railing—it was like having coffee in the center of an abandoned pagan ritual. Hazen was rocking back in his chair, dunking a scone in his coffee. He had crumbs on his shirt and his eyes were on the girl.

Thad put his coffee down. "We're still in. I just need to know that it'll be worth our time."

"Of course. More than ever. The Amish are industrious people. We can basically name our price here. Money is no concern for this man's clientele."

"I've been thinking about the antlers, and I think I know how to do it. We'll be able to bring out a small mountain of the damn things in one shot if it goes right," Thad said.

"Horses then."

"You know how they used to get logs out of the mountains back in the day, before trucks?"

"Horses and carts, I assume?"

"No. Forget the damn horses. The river. They used to float the logs out on rivers. And that's what we're going to do. If we had a couple rafts, we could load them up and paddle out at night. We could float right from the park to our backyard. Would probably take us two nights. I think it's our best shot at not getting caught. But—"

"If I'm not mistaken, there is a canyon or two that stands in between you and your backyard."

"Yeah. We have to run the canyons. There's going to be a window of time where it's doable. Right now the river is as low as it will be all year; it wouldn't be too much of a problem. Of course, there's still too much snow up there to get the antlers in the first place. How I figure it, there'll be a week where the snow is off enough for us to get in there and pick up the goods but the river won't be fully blown out. It'll probably be dicey, but I think it's the best way."

In the Scot's hands, his coffee mug looked like an espresso cup. His gun strapped to his side looked like a toy. From Thad's perspective, it was like he made everything he touched, or simply stood beside, look out of scale, like he was the size a man should be but he had somehow found himself in a dollhouse world, and had made an ironic mastery of it.

"A bold plan. One that would not have occurred to me. How do you propose to get the rafts into the backcountry without attracting attention?"

Thad gave him the gist of what he had planned so far. He thought that they would carry the rafts in under the cover of darkness, inflate and hide them. They'd scout out the area where the elk drop their antlers and start gathering. When they'd found enough, all they would have to do was load the rafts up at night and go. He didn't think going through town would be a problem. The bridge was high enough you'd have to be stopped and looking down to see anything. And it would be dark anyway. He wasn't worried about getting caught. His main worry involved navigating the canyon. And even that wouldn't be too bad if they did it right.

"We'll line the rafts down through the worst spots," Thad said. "I know there are some areas where the canyon is too steep to get out and we'll just have to go for it, but I think if we lash the boats together we could get through just about anything. I'm considering this to be a trial run. The stuff we can get out of the park is pretty much limitless; I mean, what do you think you could get for a full-curl ram's head? There's people that would pay out the nose for one of those. We could probably get that for you, bear too, maybe even a wolf or two if we got lucky and could find one without a collar. What do you think a grizzly's gallbladder would go for? One of those is probably twice the size of the black bear's we got you. Big medicine. I bet those people over there would go crazy for them. The river solves a lot of problems. It saves time, and we don't have to risk hiking out with a rifle and a pack full of shit."

The Scot sat, tapping his knee. Then he smiled wide. "Christ. I love it," he said. He abruptly stood and brushed crumbs from his kilt. "It's settled, then. Call me when you're back."

Thad rose to leave, but Hazen remained seated. He pointed at the arrangement in the vase on the table, the long, black-striped pheasant tail feathers, the holly berries so red they seemed artificially made. He spoke to the girl. "Did you make that?"

The girl nodded. The Scot smiled and patted her knee. "A woman is what makes a house a home. I've always said it."

Thad motioned to Hazen that it was time to go. He was leading the way down the steps when he heard Hazen stop and turn. "We're not in any big hurry. If she wanted to play us a song on those bagpipes, we'd be glad to stick around and hear it."

"Did you hear that, darling? You've a request for a tune."

The girl was clearing the table. She had the cups and cream and sugar on a tray. She looked at Hazen, then at her father. She gave a short shake of her head and then turned and went into the house.

OVERNIGHT IT SEEMED THE LOW HILLS TURNED FROM brown to green. The cottonwood buds were soft and gray, ready to pop. With another advance from the Scot, Thad bought two patched-up, but still serviceable, fourteen-foot self-balers, paddles, a foot pump, and life jackets from one of the rafting companies in town. At the hardware store he bought two new headlamps, extra batteries, two long lines of good rope, four camouflage-patterned tarps. This unusual burst of consumerism was thrilling but somewhat exhausting as well. He'd never before purchased so much at one time, and after it was done he had to go home and take a nap.

They spread out their father's old topo maps of the park and drank endless cups of coffee, arguing the fine points of various trailheads in relation to where they imagined the sheds would be thickest. Hazen said he knew a spot, someplace he'd come across on one of his occasional solo camping trips. It was a long open valley with a creek that held enough water to float a raft and where the antlers were scattered around like fallen leaves. At least that's what he said, and Thad was inclined to believe him. It wasn't the sort of thing his brother would make up.

There was a brief warm spell that burned off most of the high-country snow. The river spiked, raging muddy and brown. Then, a week of cold weather that made it drop and clear. As good of a time as any. The day before they were set to leave, Thad drove up the river road and then did a slow loop back toward home. The road ran the lip of the canyon, hugging the contours of the river from above. Occasionally he could see the blue-green shade of its flow between the trees. It was hard to get a finger on, but lately the river had looked different to him; the possibilities it offered rendered its walls darker, more shadowed and unfamiliar.

At two in the morning Hazen stood bleary-eyed at the kitchen counter smearing peanut butter and honey on bread. Thad had one thermos filled with coffee and was dumping grounds in the filter to brew another.

"I wish we wouldn't have run out of jerky," Hazen said. "Peanut butter sandwiches get old."

"Those sandwiches are going to taste like the best thing you ever ate after we've hauled those rafts back in there ten miles or so."

"I guess. You nervous?"

"About what? Nothing to be nervous about yet. This is just setup. Even if we did get stopped, there's nothing they can do. We're just getting exercise, training for an expedition down the Nile, or some damn thing. No laws about carrying rafts around in Yellowstone. So no, not nervous. Yet. Plenty of time for that when we actually float out. Save your nervous for then."

"Oh, I'm not nervous. I don't get nervous. I was just asking if you were."

Thad filled the other thermos with coffee, dumped in a liberal amount of sugar, and sealed the cap tight. "This stuff's going to be like liquid gold come midnight when we're still out there scrambling around."

Hazen licked the knife clean and began slapping the bread together into sandwiches. "I was thinking," he said. "Lots of thick brush. Those bears are going to be out. It's that time of year. Sows with cubs and all the rest."

"I'd thought of that too. So remember what I just said about being nervous?"

"Yeah."

"Never mind that. You can be nervous now. In the dark with the grizzlies. That makes me a little nervous."

Last night, Thad had taken the old beat-up twelve-gauge pump gun with the cracked stock that no one used anymore and put it in the vise on the workbench. Their father had shot ducks with it when he was a kid, right behind the high school, in the slough where Fleshman Creek dumps into the river. He sawed the rusted barrel off two inches past the grip and knocked down the rough edges of the cut with a file. He took a roll of duct tape and wrapped and rewrapped the split stock and then tied a cord from butt to barrel so he could wear it slung over his back. He had looked at it there in the dim light of the workshop, sitting on the bench, a crude, hackneyed tool. He'd put it on the porch untested. Now, finishing up his coffee, looking down the driveway in the dark, he took up the gun and racked in a single round of 00 buckshot in the chamber, pointed out toward the edge of the cottonwoods, and fired once from the hip. The gun recoiled so violently he almost dropped it. A sharp burst of blue-orange flame spit into the darkness from the shortened barrel, the heavy shot ripping through the new leaves and thwacking into trunks. He racked the gun once more and ejected the smoking shell.

At the sound of the shot, Hazen emerged, sandwich in hand.

"What the hell?"

Thad held up the modified gun and shrugged. "Thought I should test it out."

"No fair. You get a shotgun. What do I get?"

"You get to stay close to me. Finish up with those sandwiches. Let's go."

As they were heading out the door, Sacajawea emerged from her room.

"Was that a gunshot?"

Thad ignored her and headed for the truck. He heard Hazen tell her they were going camping. It was just for the bears.

They loaded the packs on top of the deflated rafts in the pickup bed and made it to the trailhead an hour before first light. They unloaded the gear and piled it in the headlight glare. They'd chosen this trailhead because it was seldom used, a small clearing surrounded by dense timber. A trail that led into the deep backcountry with no immediate waterfalls or vistas to attract hikers. The truck's headlights shot out into the trunks and did strange things to the trees. The lower parts of the trunks were illuminated, the bark gray in the lights, but where the light began to falter, the trees seemed to stretch on, up and up, disappearing into the black sky, overshadowing the truck. Trees like skyscrapers, like celestial tent pegs pounded into the earth to hold the black tarp of the sky in place.

Thad went into the timber, cut two small lodgepoles, dragged them back to the clearing, and stripped their branches. He laid the poles parallel and tied a short section of rope around each end so that the poles couldn't be spread more than shoulder width apart. He lashed the paddles to the tops of the poles and then had Hazen help him lift the whole thing over the raft bundles. He tied the rafts to the poles, and they lifted it to see how it would work. Hazen was in the front, Thad in the back, the poles on their shoulders with the uninflated rafts suspended in the middle. It was heavy but manageable. Loaded down, they set out down the trail that wound through the trees thin as a black hair threaded between the teeth of a comb. The small shafts of light from their headlamps were quickly swallowed by the timber. The air carried differently at night, damp, cool, and close. After not much more than a mile, the trail started to gain elevation. They continued on, leaning into the uphills, their strides matched evenly, nearly synchronized. Though they couldn't see it through the trees, the sun must have come up. Everything went slowly from black to gray-green, and then they were able to switch off their headlamps. They stopped and lowered the load and Thad wrapped his extra shirt around one pole and his rain jacket around the other. Hazen did the same and they continued on. The padding helped a little but not much. The bark rubbing under the weight of the load was going to turn the tops of their shoulders raw. It was an awkward and lurching way to travel. They came across several windfallen trees and had to negotiate their way over, straining to lift the poles up high enough so the rafts would clear the trunks. After one of these, Hazen said, "I guess it goes without saying, this blows."

"I don't think you'd even have to mention it."

"This is how the aborigines carry their kill back to camp after they've been hunting. Did you know that? They tie up a pig or whatever by the hooves and thread a pole through the legs and carry it upside down this way. They use those poison arrows, so sometimes the pig isn't even dead, just knocked out."

"Yeah, I know. I looked at all the same *National Geographic*s you did."

"I guess. These rafts are probably heavy as four pigs."

"And we don't even have any topless tribeswomen waiting for our triumphant return."

When they'd gone a few miles, they came to the river and a footbridge that hung thirty feet over the water. Thad had worried about this segment of the hike. There was a railing on one side of the bridge, and the other side was open. They hugged the railing and went carefully. They could hear the river below them, and the smell of its breath rose up to them, wet rocks and snowmelt coursing through the roots of the pines. A misstep here and everything would end, horrifically, before it had even gotten started.

"Easy," Thad said. "Slow down."

Hazen grunted but slowed, and they made it without incident. After resting for a moment on the other side, they continued. The trail began to climb again until they reached a flat grassy plain with the humped shapes of buffalo grazing in the distance. Steam rose from the thermal vents dotting the meadow. Some in steady columns of sulfurous air like smoke from a fire, others like ragged exhalations. A small group of bison, spooked by the presence of this strange four-legged beast, thundered out and away from the trail, leaving behind their rank dust. With the steam and the dust and the weak light of the sun barely forcing through the layers of pewter nimbostratus, everything seemed hazy, a cloudy cataract world.

The plain was shaped like a giant triangle whose edges were formed on one side by the big river that they'd crossed and on the other side by the smaller tributary that forced its way through Hellroaring Canyon to its eventual confluence with the main river. They struck out across the plain toward the upper reaches of the tributary, where it spilled, snow fed, out of the mountains. Already they were seeing elk. Herds of fifty or more, some bedded down in the new grass that stood out in neon-green relief against the patches of windblown snow. Hazen pointed to the elk, made an I-told-you-so gesture. At the upper end of the massive meadow, where scrub trees began to grow, stunted alder and willow and aspen, the trail became diffuse and branched out into narrow lanes favored by the elk, who had spent the winter here out of the wind, digging for grass and browsing on the shoots of the young trees. Soon progress became difficult; the brush was too thick to bash through with the rafts on the poles. They were close enough to the creek to hear it, gathering itself for the plunge into the canyon. They dropped and dismantled their carrying rig.

Almost immediately, Hazen found an elk antler. It was at the base of a small willow, the polished antler tips glowing bone white against the reddish tree stem. When it came time for the bulls to shed their antlers in the spring, they raked them on the brush and trees to dislodge them. Generally, if one antler was found, the match was somewhere close by. Thad could only imagine that to an elk, being unbalanced with a heavy rack on just the one side must be incredibly annoying. Hazen picked up the shed, a nice branching six-point with a base as thick around as his wrist.

"Well," he said. "Here we are."

"Nice one. Only about ninety-nine more to go. You might as well start seeing what you can gather. They should be all over in this thick stuff. I'm going to scout out a good spot to stash these rafts. Don't go too far. We've got to get the boats dealt with first."

Thad made his way down to the creek. It was small here. Not much wider than the rafts themselves. They would have to load the rafts and walk them down until the flow began to pick up volume from the numerous small streams that formed this time of year from the snowmelt. He walked the banks looking for a suitable spot. He wanted to hide the rafts no more than a short drag from the water. They were going to be heavy when fully loaded, but at the same time they needed to be out of sight, even from the air. It could get ugly in a hurry if, by chance, some Park Service helicopter crew were to fly over counting wolves or something and spotted the rafts.

In the end, Thad came across a massive beaver-chewed aspen. It was one of the few large trees in area. The beavers seemed to have resented its majesty and toppled it out of spite. It was still propped up on its stump, and the broken and chewed branches formed a low canopy from which the rafts would only protrude a little. Thad figured he could cut a few more branches for cover.

Thad went to find Hazen, following the noise of him crashing in the brush. In a small clearing Hazen had started piling antlers. Already he had found a half a dozen or so, and as Thad approached, Hazen came from the trees with an antler in each hand and tossed them on the pile.

"Check this out." He led Thad on a small trail back into the willows and pointed at a patch of muddy ground. There was a grizzly print. Thad knelt and put his hand over it. Even with his fingers splayed, he was unable to span the width of the track.

"That's ugly."

"Pretty old though, I think."

"Hopefully it's long gone. I really don't want to come across that thing."

"You're the one with the shotgun. How do you think I feel?"

"We'll stay within earshot. Make lots of noise. It'll be fine. Let's get those rafts set up and stashed and then we start picking."

They dragged the rafts down to the cottonwood and took turns inflating them with the foot pump. Thad spread a lightweight camouflage tarp over the boats and then they cut branches, piling them over the whole setup. Thad walked fifty yards away and looked. He knew what he was looking for, and still the rafts were not easy to spot. He figured that on the off chance some confused hiker were to wander off the trail, they would pass right by the boats without ever seeing them. The effective camouflage alleviated his nerves slightly. At this point they'd veered heavily into illegality. Every year dozens of tourists were cited for removing antlers from the park, despite the warning signs posted everywhere. As far as Thad knew, arguing ignorance was not enough to dodge a fine, even for the possession of a single antler. If they got busted with a colossal pile like the one he was hoping to accumulate, he didn't want to even guess what the penalty would be.

By this time it was late afternoon. They took a sandwich break, sitting on rocks by the creek. They drank a thermos of coffee between them while they ate. They didn't talk much. The amount of work that still lay ahead of them was daunting. It was cool and still cloudy, the flat lead-gray kind that threatened rain or probably snow at this elevation. Rain would make things uncomfortable, but snow was a different story. Even just two inches of wet snow would coat the ground, the brush, the trees, and of course the antlers, making them all but impossible to find. If it snowed, they were screwed, no two ways about it.

Thad finished his sandwich, downed the rest of his coffee, stood and stretched, and slung the shotgun over his shoulder.

"Let's go harvest the fields," he said.

They spread three large tarps on the ground, each one a few hundred yards from the others, in a roughly triangular formation. The plan was to work the area within the tarps, scour the ground, pile the antlers on the tarps, and then, when the area had been complexly picked, drag them to a new area and start the process over again. Thad thought that if a guy had the time and the inclination to do it right, he would get a topographical map and set up a grid. Mark it out with flags or pieces of ribbon on the trees. It would take some time on the setup, but overall it would be more efficient; you wouldn't waste time going back over spots you'd already covered, and you'd be less likely to miss areas altogether. Maybe next time, if there was a next time, that's how he'd do it.

While they combed the grass and the low undergrowth for antlers, they kept within shouting distance of each other. The light was starting to fall, and with the onset of dark Thad was more worried about bears than he was about someone hearing them, so they started to make noise to warn any potential animals of their presence. Thad shouted, "Hey bear, hey bear," when he came up on a particularly thick patch of willows. He clapped his hands. Hazen whistled "Yankee Doodle Dandy." After this he sang "Happy Birthday" over and over again, cycling through the names of everyone he knew. It wasn't a long list. Several teachers from high school were there, Lil from the Goose. Their parents. Jerry from the Town Pump. Thad caught glimpses of Hazen now and again through the shadows slowly engulfing the brush. He had mud smeared on his jeans, his arms, his face. His hair was loose around his shoulders, littered with broken twigs and leaves. Two large elk antlers were wedged into his belt at the small of his back, branching over his shoulders like the wings of a skeletal bird. He held two more in one hand, and as Thad watched he bent and picked up another one. He said something under his breath that Thad couldn't hear and then headed back to dump his cargo on the tarp.

It was a cool night, and thus far the precipitation had held off. Before it got fully dark, Thad built a fire in a small clearing well away from their antler piles. It was a small fire that didn't produce much warmth. The wind had come up a little, and the fire battened down and then flared. Thad breathed in deeply of this wind coming up from the south, born of a land that harbored no people, just rocks and snow and trees and the twisting braids of rivers. It was right out there at his back, the largest tract of wilderness in the lower forty-eight, and he could feel it pushing almost like the very beginning of a migraine headache, a pressure just behind his eyes.

They collected antlers and the moon rose up like a great gold watch fob on a chain. Under their headlamps the antlers shone white and stood out in stark relief against the underbrush. In the dark their search became somewhat aimless. What few landmarks there were became unrecognizable, and they wandered, sometimes stumbling near each other, sometimes seeing their own boot tracks illuminated in a place they had no recollection of having been. Eventually, near midnight, they rolled up in their bedrolls and slept next to the fire. They could hear wolves hunting at the far end of the valley, their piercing yips of excitement, and then it was quiet.

THEY WERE UP BEFORE DAWN. ANOTHER SANDWICH. THE coffee was gone, and Thad wished he would have remembered to pack some instant. They drank water from the creek, down on hands and knees, sucking straight off the cold surface. Hazen plunged his whole head in and came up shaking like a dog, his hair sending water spraying.

"Refreshing," he said.

"I'll pass," said Thad.

They went back to work in the gray light of a new morning. Low clouds had set in, and everywhere they walked elk crashed through the brush ahead of them. In a small swale almost completely covered over in chokecherry bushes, Thad found a massive bull elk, dead and mostly decomposed, its rib bones clean and white as piano keys. It had a wide branching rack, seven points on each side, still intact and attached to a skull that had scraps of fur still clinging, eye sockets gaping ragged and empty. A bull like this was old, the dominant male, and at one time had commanded a large harem of cows. The stress of the rut last fall—the energy expended running off the younger bulls and mating the cows—had most likely weakened him, and the winter had done the rest. Thad took his knife and pounded it between the vertebrae behind the skull until it separated. He hefted the rack and skull and thought about how fine a line it was between being in the prime of life and being a pile of bones so picked over that there was no longer enough left to feed a worm. It was a good find. Antlers with the skulls attached fetched a higher price than sheds, once they'd been cleaned and polished. A taxidermist in town kept a large vat of beetles for this very purpose. He could put a fully fleshed deer or elk head into the vat, and in a week the beetles would have completely removed every scrap of fur, flesh, brain, and hide.

By now their three tarps each held a tangled mound of antlers that rose nearly head high, and each new addition meant that they were that much closer to being able to make the float out. Thad figured that each raft could safely carry six or seven hundred pounds of antlers. He wasn't sure, but he'd guess that most of the sheds they'd found were between ten and fifteen pounds, a few lighter, a few heavier. Fifty antlers per raft was the number he'd settled on, a nice even one hundred for the total.

They redoubled their efforts, moving around the game trails at a half jog. Thad had taken off his belt and used it to carry the antlers in a bundle slung over his shoulder. Hazen noticed and did the same and they scoured the brush, their backs bent under their strange crooked loads. Hazen had found a dead buffalo, a young male, its parts scattered over an area the size of a swimming pool. A leg here, a rib there, pieces of vertebrae strewn about. Probably it had been singled out and killed by wolves in the deep snow. Then the coyotes had come in after and gotten what they could. Hazen had found the skull, still rank with decaying hide and brain matter, and he'd strung it up by the short curved horns and carried it with his antler bundle done up with his belt. The hollow clunking of this assemblage preceded him through the brush. When Thad passed him, he could smell the skull, the sick sweet smell of rot. A skull like that, when given the beetle treatment and whitened with cosmetologist's peroxide, could go for three hundred dollars or more. People liked to situate them over a wall sconce so light came through the empty eye sockets and the nostrils.

"Nice find," Thad said. "You'd gag a maggot."

Hazen laughed and shrugged and headed off into a thicket of alder, the skull bumping off his back as he walked.

Toward afternoon, the antlers were getting harder to find. They'd picked an area slightly smaller than a square mile, and while there were undoubtedly still many sheds to be found, there was now a lot of walking to do between finds. They reconvened at one of the tarps and ate a sandwich. They were slightly shy of a hundred, but the antlers they'd already found would make for a large, precarious load on the rafts. Thad decided that for the first trip, they should probably not overdo it. Thad had a pretty good idea of the type of water they'd be facing on the descent, and he wasn't exactly sure how the rafts would handle it. They teamed up to drag the three antler-laden tarps down to where the rafts were stashed and transferred the loads to the boats. They mounded antlers, lashing them down securely, leaving a small clear area in each of the sterns for them to sit with a paddle.

Thad tied a rope from the stern of the first raft to the bow of the second and double-checked that their loads were secure. He pulled the camouflage tarps over the loads and tucked the loose ends under the rafts. Judging by the sun, now about to skewer itself onto a lodge-pole-covered ridge, he figured they had enough time before it was dark to scout the head of the canyon where it was wooded to see if there were any downed trees. He had a bad image of them coming around a sharp bend to find a sweeper, the rafts too heavy to slow or stop.

After the creek left the thickets of tangled alder and willow, it flowed in a meandering serpentine line through the long meadow under the gray drifting clouds of steam from the thermal vents. After the meadow, it plunged into the first of a series of canyons. When they emerged from the brush, they kept the creek within sight and made their way across the broad meadow. Throughout the previous day it had threatened to rain, but it never did; now the sky was clear blue, marred by a single white jet trail. Hazen was in the lead, and the only sound was the flowing water and their boots swishing through the low grass and the occasional creak of their pack straps. Then Hazen stopped.

"Do you think Dad would have liked what we're doing right now?" he said.

"Hiking on a nice day in the world's first national park? Why wouldn't he?" Thad motioned for Hazen to get moving, but he remained where he was.

"You know what I mean," Hazen said.

"I know. And, no, probably not. But I'm not sure; he could be funny that way. My guess is he would find it reckless, not worth the risk."

"Remember that first trip we did for the Scot, the fall before dad died?"

"Yeah."

"I told him about it. That people in Asian countries eat bear livers. I told him we made a bunch of money."

"The man is literally on his death bed and you come to him with that? What's wrong with you?"

"It's better than what you did."

"What?"

"You would have put him in his grave that first day he came back from the doctors and told us. At least I talked to him like normal. Took him fishing." Hazen was starting to say something else when Thad closed the gap between them and hit him with an open palm across the face. Hazen stumbled back, his eyes watering, his hand on his cheek. He didn't look up. He wiped at his eyes with his sleeve and charged Thad.

They fought like they hadn't since they were kids, when their father would sometimes have to separate them with a broom handle. Neither of them had shed their packs, and when Hazen's shoulder hit Thad in the midsection, they went down in a heap. Hazen was swinging wildly with his left hand, his right pinned to the ground under him. He landed a shot to the side of Thad's head that made Thad's ears ring. They fought silently, rolling and thrashing, the awkward packs making it hard for either one to get much of an advantage until Thad put his knee into Hazen's stomach. For a moment, Hazen was laid out, gasping and spitting, and it was enough time for Thad to undo the buckles on his pack, swing astride Hazen, make a double wrap of hair around his fist, and push his face into the bison-trampled ground. Hazen struggled, but the weight of his pack with Thad on top of it was too much and he went still.

"Remember how when Dad was sick, the lights stayed on? Remember how there was food in the refrigerator? That was because of me." Thad was speaking low and close to Hazen's ear. He lifted Hazen's head by the hair and thumped it on the ground. "Half the time you have no idea what goes on around you. You just live, and the rest of us have to make sure things work. I get you out of trouble you don't even know you're in. I've been doing it my whole life. If this doesn't go right, we stand to lose the house, OK? How about that?"

Hazen bucked futilely for a moment and then lay, breathing hard.

"Bullshit."

Thad thumped Hazen's head on the ground once more, for good measure, not as hard this time. "It's something called a tax lien. Now is not the time to discuss it. Are you done? If I let you up, you are done?"

Hazen nodded, his cheek still to the ground, and Thad let go of his hair and stood. Hazen heaved himself to his hands and knees and spit, his hair in his face, dirt clinging to his cheek like a bruise. He didn't look at Thad, and Thad thought he was going to come at him again. But he got to his feet and brushed at the dirt on his face with his sleeve and set out walking. After a while, Thad followed.

A lone raven drifted across the meadow, the sun making its feathers glossy as motor oil. It croaked once and was gone. Thad felt like the uneasy balance he and Hazen had been maintaining had been thrown off, maybe irrevocably. In other situations it wouldn't have been an immediate problem, but at this point Thad needed to know with some degree of certainty that he could rely on his brother. One little tiff like this could derail Hazen, push him toward further acts of impulse that could land them both in trouble. It was painful, but Thad knew that sometimes you had to swallow the bone, force it down rather than risk having it lodge. After they had hiked for a while, he took a deep breath and cleared his throat.

"I apologize," he said.

Hazen didn't acknowledge that he'd heard and so Thad let it be.

ON ITS WAY THROUGH THE MEADOW THE CREEK WAS mellow and slow-moving. Shin- to knee-deep in most places, only a few gravel bars they'd have to drag the rafts over. Thad had been worried about logjams, but the lack of trees made it a nonissue. It was still early afternoon when they reached the narrow gap where the creek poured down a small waterfall ledge and began its descent to the main river. Thad pointed at the waterfall. "That might be exciting," he said. Hazen didn't reply. He hadn't spoken to Thad since the fight. It might be a while before he did.

They stood looking down the creek as far as they could, which wasn't very far, as the canyon made a sharp bend not too far downstream. The sound of the water was a loud omnipresent force here, pulsing in an almost arterial manner. Like the roar of blood in your ears when you're in an absolutely silent place, Thad thought, like somewhere deep in the granite a mountain heart was pumping its icy flow. There was something about nature that was twice told. The human vascular system resembled the drainages of mountains, resembled the branching prongs of a lightning strike resembled the xylem and phloem of trees from roots all the way to the lacework veins of the leaves. It was something Thad had thought about but had never been able to pin down. In the fall, the red and gold and copper of the streamside alders and cottonwoods and willows were reflected in the spawning colors of the brown trout. It was almost enough to instill some sort of faith in a creator, some sort of guiding hand, an artist with a limited palette. Things were so remarkably similar when it seemed like they should be more different. When stripped of hide and hair, a bear's skeleton looked eerily like a human form. The colors of certain sunsets were the colors of fire devouring wood, the sparks sent up to the sky perfect replicas of stars. Maybe it meant something; maybe it didn't. The human mind was a register of patterns. Whether or not those patterns existed outside the brain itself was another matter altogether.

They stood on the edge of the canyon, and the rock transmitted the roar of the water up through their boots, up their feet and shins and knees and thighs before reaching their guts, the deep vibration curling up there and settling. They could smell the water, crushed upon the rocks and vaporized, rising up to meet them.

"Well," Thad said eventually. "I guess it doesn't look too bad."

Hazen had wandered off. He was sitting on a rock facing the trees. His back was to Thad and the river.

They followed the canyon for another few miles until the way became impassable. As far as Thad could see, there was going to be a couple spots where they were going to have to line the rafts down with the rope, but for the most part it looked like they'd be able to ride it out. Of course, there was still a substantial section before the creek entered the river that they hadn't seen. They didn't have time to scout the whole length. They'd seen what they could, and all they could do was hope for the best.

On their way back to where they'd stashed the rafts, Hazen, in the front, crested a small rise and immediately dropped to his stomach, pulling Thad down with him. Hazen pointed over the hill. "People," he said.

Thad crawled to where he could see. There were four men on horses coming across the meadow, heading to the creek. They wore olive-drab Park Service uniforms with Kevlar vests. They had guns on their hips and shotguns in scabbards attached to their saddles. All of them were staring at the ground, riding slowly, still almost a mile out.

All Thad could feel was a tingling around his periphery. His heart thumping into the ground underneath him. "We're fucked," he said. They could probably get to the boats well before the men could get across the valley, but there was no way the men wouldn't see them floating.

"We could just go home," Hazen said. "Circle back around and get the truck and go."

"We could do that. They'd find the rafts." Thad felt his mind spinning, turning the problem over and over, no good solutions available other than one long shot. "I wasn't making that up about losing the house. That's real. If we hustle, we might be able to get to the canyon before they get to the creek," he said.

Hazen pursed his lips. "I don't see how someone can just take the house from us."

"They could just wait for us at the bridge in town," Thad said. "Nail us there. But what if we stop before then, stash the stuff, and hike out? We might be able to slip away. Get the antlers later. Fuck, I don't know. What do you think?"

Hazen shrugged. "You should have told me. I live there too."

Not for the first time, Thad wished Hazen might have an original, helpful, idea. It was a foolish hope. A waste of time. He might as well have been talking to himself. Thad watched the men's slow progress, clock ticking in his mind. "Goddamn it," he said. "Let's try."

They cut back toward the creek and made their way through the brush as quickly as they could. They got to the rafts, and Thad wormed his way on his stomach to a point he could see. The men had come closer but were still a ways out. Moving carefully, scanning the ground for tracks, about to enter a dense stand of lodgepoles.

"You think they even know we're here?" Hazen said.

"Too much of a coincidence for it to be otherwise. I think they know we're in the area but don't know exactly where, so they're being cautious."

"How could they know?"

"I have an idea, but it doesn't really matter at this point. Let's go."

WHEN IT CAME DOWN TO IT, THE WHOLE THING SEEMED fairly ridiculous. Sure, they'd shot some bears. They had gathered up some sheds that, left undisturbed, would be chewed by the mice and the porcupines, would eventually break down and decompose into nothing. It was like having an apple orchard and not wanting the fruit but at the same time denying access to those who would gladly go in and make use of it. How was it illegal to gather that which gravity has drawn to the earth? It was a good line, but Thad didn't think it would hold up in court. Thad turned to look at Hazen. "If we get caught, don't admit to a damn thing."

"You think we're going to get caught?"

"I'm just trying to cover all the possibilities. Don't say anything, and I'll take the rap. It was my idea. Both of us have clean records. We've been facing financial difficulties. Just experienced a death in the family. We'll play it like that, and we'll probably get some community service and a fine. They might take our hunting privileges away."

Hazen looked off to the horizon over Thad's shoulder. "I've been thinking on it some more, and I think Dad would think that this was pretty great. There might be no one that's ever done this before. I think it's something he'd like to hear about. That we pulled it off."

"We haven't pulled it off."

"I'm just saying. Remember how he didn't buy a fishing or hunting license that last year?"

"He was dying. State-sponsored licensing procedures seemed kind of irrelevant," Thad said.

"I think he thought that all along. He never voted."

"I've never voted."

"Me either."

"I don't know how the world keeps turning."

Thad tossed Hazen a life jacket. He checked the loads one more time to make sure everything was secure. Before pushing off, he dropped the old, disfigured shotgun into the creek. Thad didn't feel right about just chucking it. Still, the gun wasn't registered, and having it on them could only add to their problems. The water—snow, not too long ago—was freezing cold when it seeped into their boots. Thad manhandled the lead boat into the creek and then hopped in. The current caught the raft and the rope came taut and pulled the second raft along behind it, and then

Hazen, giving a final push, jumped into the second raft and they were on their way.

They floated out of the brushy upper section of the creek and soon were in the long meandering meadow. The streambed was narrow here; they didn't so much paddle as they did use the paddles to push off the banks and rocks and deadfall. They were exposed. There was little in the way of bankside vegetation, and Thad's scalp prickled. He wanted the creek to move faster. He tried to use the paddle like a punt pole to move them along, but it didn't make much difference.

They rounded the last bend before the creek dumped into the canyon. The brush cleared, affording them a view of the meadow. A quarter of a mile away, the men on horseback were emerging from the trees, heading straight for the creek. There was nothing to do but float. Events had been set in motion, and all that was left was to see how they played out. The men were clearly following their tracks, looking at the ground, pausing every once in a while to scan the meadow ahead of them. Steam rose white and thick as foul-smelling pipe smoke. Thad watched, hardly breathing, as the men picked their way around the steam vents and buffalo wallows. They stopped, and he could see them gesturing. One of the men turned and pointed at the creek, or maybe the mountain behind it, and Thad thought for sure that they had been spotted. They were in plain sight. All the men had turned and were facing up the creek. One of them had binoculars out, and the sun flashed off the lenses. Thad and Hazen were frozen, not paddling, the rafts nosing downstream of their own accord, the water slapping loudly against the rubber.

To Thad it seemed that the men were staring directly at them, but they made no signs or gestures or yells, and then they turned and continued on heading upstream.

Thad exhaled the breath he'd been holding. Hazen let out a quiet whistle. Thad turned and scanned the hill behind them. It wasn't long before he spotted what the men had actually been looking at. There was a bear, an old boar with a silver ruff of fur on its shoulders. He was several hundred yards away on the side of a hill with his back to the creek, using both paws to rip up a rotted stump, looking for grubs. The bear had broad powerful haunches and shoulders, its fur rippling as pieces of bark and wood flew. The men had naturally turned upstream to avoid crossing paths with this beast, and in doing so had completely missed the brothers floating by.

"Bears are my spirit animal," Hazen said, making a clawing motion with his hands.

Thad laughed and shook his head. For the first time since they'd spotted the men on horseback, he was able to breathe normally. "I think we're in the clear," he said. "I think we're good."

As they neared the mouth of the canyon, the creek began to pick up speed. The rafts hawed against the rope that tied them together, and on several occasions Thad and Hazen had to push off protruding rocks with their boots to keep from getting hung up. They were both wet from the knee down. Thad's feet ached from the cold, and the joints of his fingers felt stiff from the frigid water dripping down the paddles. When the canyon walls closed around them, the temperature dropped ten degrees. The sun was out of sight below the west rim, and the creek dashing against the rocks reincarnated as cold humidity. Almost immediately after entering, the creek formed a short rock-ledge waterfall. The rafts dropped over it one after another, slapping down bow first, hardly taking on any water at all. Thad could hear Hazen whooping as he went over. To a person used to traveling in the backcountry by foot, floating seemed amazingly fast and, other than the cold, comfortable. No heavy packs digging into your shoulders, no blisters on your feet: just sit on your ass and let the water do the work.

He turned back to Hazen and said, "This isn't so bad."

"Huh?"

"I said, I could get used to this." He gestured with his paddle and then realized that he'd just yelled at the top of his lungs and Hazen could barely hear him. Since entering the canyon, the noise of the creek had been a steady dull roar, but almost imperceptibly it had gotten even louder, a constant crashing that filled the narrow space between the canyon walls, the noise as palpable as the water itself. Thad faced forward, and they rounded a corner, and the creek ahead was a roiling mass of frothy white. There was no time to stop and scout the best route, no way to halt the rafts' forward progress even if they wanted to. The boats seemed to leap into the fray. The first wave in an endless chain broke over the bow, and instantly Thad was soaked through, his hair plastered to his forehead. He had his feet wedged under the raft thwart and was paddling with everything he had. He had no idea if the paddling was making any difference at all. The rafts seemed incredibly sluggish and heavy. The creek was dropping elevation quickly, and now the canyon loomed above them, the walls a striated blur as they careened past. Each corner they rounded brought more of the same, the spray of piercingly cold water, the pitching and tossing of the rafts bucking through the rollers, sliding over rocks and pinballing off the canyon walls. Thad's hands felt like they were fused to the paddle shaft. Every so often, he turned to make sure Hazen was still there. He was, his lips pulled back on his teeth in a grimace as he paddled.

It was getting dark, and when they came to a section where the creek slowed, they pulled over. There was a small gravel beach, and Thad ran the bow of his raft aground and hopped out to pull Hazen in. He almost fell face-first but caught himself in a stumble against the raft. His legs were numb, and he had to sit and wait for blood to return. They pulled the rafts up the gravel, and while Thad retied the load of antlers, which had shifted in the rapids, Hazen scrambled up a steep crevasse in the canyon walls that held several large sections of trees washed down from runoff in years past.

The wood was damp, and they had a hard time getting a blaze going. Eventually it took, and they huddled around the smoky fire, trying to dry themselves. Hazen was shaking, his teeth chattering together audibly. Thad threw more wood on, and gradually they began peeling off layers and spreading them out on forked sticks to dry. They hunched, naked, alternately turning to warm their fronts and backs. Hazen made a knot of his hair and wrung it over the fire in a hiss of steam. Their bedrolls were soaked through. They were out of food, and they didn't talk. The river filled the silence. Eventually Thad put on his smoke-dried clothes and dozed, leaning back against the bow of a raft. The fire cast its flickering light on the canyon walls, and the shadows in the crevasses and crags appeared like glyphs, fantastic animals and humanoid forms with alien proportions.

Thad had seen actual rock art. There were caves above the river where the drawings and scratchings were still faintly visible. Their father had taken them up there when they were old enough to climb the steep rock faces and still young enough to allow themselves to be haunted by ghosts. As far as Thad knew, the caves were undiscovered by archaeologists and the like. They were small and probably not places where people had ever lived. The access route was too difficult for everyday living, and most of the caves were too low-ceilinged to stand. The rock was blackened from fire, and the drawings were rough-hewn and imagistic. Basic shapes, handprints in ocher, things that resembled deer or elk, wavy lines and jagged etchings that may have been rivers, mountains. These were spooky places, cramped and dry and smelling of Rodentia. The sites overlooked the river, and Thad had no way of knowing but he thought that maybe in ancient days men had come there to seek some sort of spiritual intervention in their lives. To sit and tend a small fire and wait for the dawn to watch the sun rise over the river, solitary in its position as they themselves were in theirs.

Hazen tossed a branch onto the fire. Sparks rose. They would rest here until the moon became visible in the slice of sky between the canyon walls; some light was better than none, and then they would push the rafts into the cold current and continue on.

NOT LONG AFTER THEIR STOP AT THE SMALL BEACH, the creek emptied itself into the main river. The channel deepened, and the relatively calm sections between rapids were longer, the rapids themselves more intense. At one point Thad could feel the raft pitching forward underneath him, and in the moonlight he could see downstream the river dropping from ledge to ledge, as steeply as a set of crooked stairs. He yelled at Hazen and redoubled his efforts with the paddle. They managed to get the rafts pulled into a long eddy formed by a large boulder. Thad hopped out in water up to his knees and pulled the rafts in to shore. He thought that they could probably ride out the next section, but he could not see enough of it to be sure. The safe thing was to tie the long rope to the rear raft and line the boats down through. They made sure the loads were secure and then, stumbling on the rocky banks, walked downstream in and out of the frigid water while the rafts bobbed through waves, bounced off rocks, and scraped along the bedrock ledges that formed the rapids. The rafts were soon out of sight in the dark, and it was all they could do to keep the rope in hand while they clambered after.

While scrambling after the rafts, the rope coiled around his wrist, Thad slipped on an algae-covered rock and fell hard. There was shock. A sharp crack. Searing pain in his forearm. He kept scrambling along. Eventually the rage of the water began to subside, and the boats, still out of sight, stopped tugging so hard on their leash. Thad and Hazen made their way on the rocks, fallen from the canyon rim, until the rafts came in sight, floating peacefully at the head of a large calm pool. It looked like the antler loads were still intact. Thad was too cold and numb to even feel much relief.

Back in the raft he saw blood glistening purple when his headlamp moved across the thwart. The pain in his arm hadn't been too bad at first, but now he trained his lamp on it and could see through the rip in his jacket a large, partially detached flap of skin. When he gingerly pushed the flap aside, he could see the greenish white flash of bone. His stomach churned. There was blood everywhere, making his hands slick, beading up and forming rivulets on the waterproof jacket. He turned and yelled to Hazen. He dug with stiff fingers for his pack. He had a pair of spare socks, and when he found them he tried to tie one around his forearm, but it was awkward and hard to do with one hand.

Hazen hopped from boat to boat and helped him, forming a double wrap and knot with the sock, which immediately reddened. Hazen was saying something to him, but Thad was having a hard time hearing. The roar of water was ever-present and all-encompassing, and in a strange way it was now closer to absolute silence than noise. Thad could hardly hear the sound of the water, but he couldn't hear anything else either. Hazen was talking, or at least his mouth was moving, and he had blood on his hands too, and he wiped them on his jeans, still saying something. "Are you OK? Are you OK?" But things were getting dangerously dim around the edges of Thad's vision. Lack of food, loss of blood, not much sleep in days. The headlamp wasn't helping either. There was a cone of light outside of which everything was a question. Tunnel vision and an absurd amount of blood.

"OK," Thad said. "I'm OK." He motioned for Hazen to get back to his raft.

They floated on and he struggled to keep his grip, one-handed, on the paddle. He tried to remember if there were major arteries in the forearm. How many pints of blood were in the human body? There was a hollowness dead center in his chest, right under the rib cage. He knew it was impossible, but he imagined it was his heart gasping and sucking like a pump running dry.

He had a conversation with his father. He may have been talking out loud, or it may have been in his head. His father was telling him in great detail the error of his ways.

See? Cutting wood is downright honorable compared to this giant campaign of idiocy. You could be at home just waking up for a long day in the woods. Honest labor where you might earn yourself a few calluses and build a few muscles. At the end of the day you have a pile of wood. A tangible thing that you can receive payment and respect for. A day-in and day-out endeavor. Not to mention you could see that your brother makes out OK. And you could afford to put some shingles on the damn roof.

Thad hadn't ever really prayed. They'd never gone to church, and if someone had asked him about his beliefs in God he would have had a hard time articulating them. Thad had a general idea, and it came down to particles. No matter on earth could ever be truly destroyed or created, only changed. He remembered that from science class. Where consciousness came from he wasn't sure except that in the end it was nothing more than a byproduct of the unique arrangement of molecules. And if this was the case, then other arrangements of molecules—trees, grass, rocks—had something like a consciousness that was inherent in them, and all these things were connected, because at some point all matter was part of the same piece. All there is was all there ever was. No more, no less. Time didn't exist, and God was everything, including humans, and since this was the case, why worship? Did fingers worship the hand? That's what Thad thought, and even so, it didn't stop him, not so much from praying as from making a bargain with the assemblage of particles that had once been his father. If he made it out of there, the first thing he was going to do was fix the roof. And no more fucking around on the gray edges of illegality. He would go out and cut a mountain's worth of firewood. He screamed it out. A solemn promise. But if his father heard, he made no sign. There was just the churning roar of the creek and the airborne spray of the cold water, and then just as dawn was about to break they emerged from the canyon, the rafts merged with the main river, and at least for a while the water was tranquil. The noise subsided. It was like a blindfold being lifted. Thad heard a bird chirp. Nearly hypothermic and bone weary, they pulled over.

THAD WAS LYING IN THE DARK ON THE EDGE OF THE river, in the wet sand. He was holding his injured arm close to his body. He tried to burrow a depression in the sand for his shoulder, and as he shifted himself on the ground he heard Hazen coughing. When they were kids, their father had constantly cautioned them against the dangers of "wearing yourself out." What this meant was not that they shouldn't work hard or exhaust themselves physically; it was more of a warning about the dangers of doing things in a manner that caused unnecessary wear and tear on the body. When lifting a heavy chunk of wood to be split, you used your knees, not your back. When swinging a maul all day it was important to incorporate the legs and hips, not just the arms and shoulders. Packs should be adjusted properly and not overloaded. Don't work with dull tools of any kind, chainsaws, knives, axes, fishing hooks even.

Wearing oneself out was not a testament to a man's capacity for work—it was a symptom of his ignorance. Or, in a seemingly contradictory situation, laziness. Sometimes the man working the hardest, the guy who constantly "wears himself out," is the laziest, unwilling to take the time on the front end to do things the right way. He had always had this idea that as you aged and became a man, you became more concerned with doing things the right way. As a child, you leave your bike lying in the yard, as a teenager your room is a mess and there is a pile of smelly fishing gear in the back of your truck, but, at some undetermined point, all this is left behind for a new way of living. Responsible manhood. A knife-sharpening, gear-cleaning, firewood-stacking, roof-fixing, money-stockpiling existence. Every fall he made sure there was enough meat in the freezer to get them through the winter. If something broke on the truck, he usually managed to get it fixed without hiring it out. These things he'd learned from his father, and they were easy to perpetuate, but the bigger picture—that was a different story. He sat up and gingerly repositioned the blood-soaked sock around his arm. He was wearing himself out; there was no way to deny it. He'd been doing it for a long time. Getting mixed up with the Scot and before that even, peddling single loads of cut firewood around town. His father had always told him that if he was smart he'd take the wood up to Big Sky and charge the second-home, ski-vacation crowd an arm and a leg. He'd never done it, though. He'd been working hard, true, but no amount of expended effort can make fruitful the worker who toils aimlessly.

It was light now, and even though the sun wouldn't climb the canyon walls for several hours it felt warmer. Hazen built a small fire and they huddled, drying out slowly.

"How's the arm?" Hazen had his legs crossed and was holding his shirt over the fire, his torso bare and pale.

"Hurts like a bitch."

"Want me to look at it?"

"No."

"Probably will need some stitches."

"I think it's broken."

"Can you move it?"

"Not much."

"Did we pack a first aid kit?"

"I have no idea. Doesn't matter."

"How far do you think we have to go?"

"Day and a half probably.

"That's what I figured."

"Then why'd you ask?"

"Just making conversation."

"Well don't feel like you have to on account of me."

Thad was slumped, half asleep. It felt like two strong hands were pushing him down by the shoulders. He was throbbing. There was a steady pulse of pain that started in his arm but seemed to spread throughout his body. The arm was the epicenter, but there was no part of him that remained untouched. The pain was rhythmic and in sync with the pulse in his veins. He vomited. A greenish stream of water and bile. He hadn't been able to turn his head in time, and most of it landed in his lap, further polluting his already-foul jeans. Sitting up was suddenly unbearable. He slumped further until he tilted and met the ground in a thump, his head almost landing in the fire. The last thing he remembered was Hazen leaping up to slap at the flames that smoldered and curled the tips of his hair.

The river, the canyon, the pitching and tossing of the rapids, the long stretches of calm. The night with the moon like a perfect round auger hole bored into the sky. A hole through which one could pass into a world where everything was gleaming alabaster and silent as the bottom of the ocean. In Thad's state he climbed through this portal and sat with his legs dangling over the edge. He could see it all happening below him. Hazen dragging him into the raft, pulling the rafts into the current, and riding out of control through the serpentine canyon's flow. He could hear the rub of the rubber on the canyon wall, hear the suck and pull of water coming and receding through the raft's self-bailing floor. It sounded to him like the breathing of an elk, shot through the lungs and gasping wetly as it knelt to its final bed in the red-soaked grass. Sometimes he could hear Hazen talking, singing. He sang "The Star-Spangled Banner," and apparently he'd forgotten all the verses except for the first because he repeated it over and over, transitioning into "Black Betty," by Ram Jam, a song something like this: "Oh say can you see by the stars' early light, o'er the ramparts we watched hey Black Betty, bam ba lam." At some point the singing was done and Hazen began whistling with the .22 shell, a fluctuating pitch that rose and dropped and then climbed until Thad, perched on the edge of the moon and also flat on his back in the bottom of the freezing-cold raft, succumbed to the waves of pain and went under again.

THINGS HAD GOTTEN MESSY. THERE WAS NO OTHER WAY to put it. Hazen had saved his ass. That was undeniable. Thad's overall memories of the event were hazy. He'd gone into shock, was losing blood, and very well could have died. Apparently, Hazen had run the rest of the canyon solo. He ditched the raft he'd been riding in and climbed into Thad's. As he floated, he cut the tiedowns and started pushing antlers into the river, so that by the time he came under the bridge at the park boundary it was just him and a paddle, Thad unconscious on the floor of the raft.

They were there on the bridge, waiting. A spotlight pinned the rafts to the black river, and Hazen raised his arms over his head, waved his paddle, screamed that they needed help. As it turned out, instead of arresting them, the Fish, Wildlife and Parks officers and the game warden waiting there scrambled down the bank and hoisted Thad out, raced him to the hospital.

Thad had been barely responsive through the whole hospital visit. He did remember at one point thinking that the whole thing was going to be very, very expensive. After his father's ordeal, Thad had planned on getting basic health insurance, for himself and Hazen both, but he hadn't gotten around to it. Another stupid decision to add to the list of stupid decisions he'd made over the past year. He had a compound fracture.

Two days later they released him. While he was still in a near coma from the painkillers, the cops showed up with the game warden and questioned the two of them together, then separately. They searched the house and the grounds. Thad was fully expecting to get led away in handcuffs but was too exhausted and sore to really care. In the end, the officers found nothing. Thad could barely form coherent answers. When they interrogated Hazen in a separate room, Thad could hear him rambling and laughing, and eventually the officers emerged shaking their heads and shrugging.

In the end, they got a fine for illegal boating in Yellowstone National Park. The officer in charge had casually known their father and had heard of his passing. The officer told them that they were lucky bastards. "I know what you were up to, and I suggest you change your ways," he said before leaving. He pointed at Thad. "Don't push your luck."

After the officers left, Hazen sat down at the table across from Thad. They were quiet for a moment, and then Hazen took the .22 shell out of his shirt pocket and tapped it on the table a few times before speaking. "I thought you might die in the canyon," he said. "I was trying to figure out what I'd do."

"Yeah? What was your plan?"

"I thought that if you died, I would just keep floating. Dump you and the antlers and go all the way."

"All the way where?"

"Down the Yellowstone. To the Missouri. The Mississippi. All the way to the Gulf."

"Sorry to disappoint you. Next time I'll die and you can be Huck Finn."

"I'm just saying. I hadn't thought much about you dying before. I mean, I had a plan in place. I was going to roll your body into the river and just keep going."

"Is there something you're trying to say here?"

"Not really."

"Nothing's different."

"Things are different. I'd never considered you dying, like truly, as a real possibility, and then I did. And now things are different."

"OK," Thad said. "I guess we'll figure it out. Now I'm tired, and I'm going to sleep for the next several days."

"I'm talking about me." Hazen looked out the window and cracked his knuckles loudly. "I want to get my own truck," he said.

Thad got up from the table and stretched and yawned. "It was smart of you to ditch the antlers," he said. "It was the right move." He left Hazen sitting there looking out the window, smiling around the .22 shell pursed between his lips.

Weeks later, walking by *The Enterprise* box outside County Market, Thad caught a headline: "POACHED!" He bought a copy. Several men in a local "ring" had gotten busted in the middle of the night, their homes searched. Trials pending, they faced having their hunting and fishing privileges stripped for life by the state of Montana. Fines upward of one hundred thousand dollars. Up to a year in jail. The Scot was not among the names of the men indicted, and Thad knew how it had probably gone. The Scot got caught with something, made a deal. Served the others up on a platter in exchange for reduced charges. Several times Thad drove by his driveway and the gate was always closed and locked, new grass growing in the two-track up to the house. A couple names in that newspaper story were men from local families Thad would not want to be crosswise with. He'd heard that the Scot and his daughter had moved. Not to Scotland but Columbus, Ohio, where the Scot was from originally.

IT WAS THE SUMMER THAT NEVER WAS. LONG STRETCHES of gray cool days, nights in early August where Thad could see his breath. The Fourth of July rodeo was held on a blustery afternoon where the sun made only a brief appearance, and those that stuck around to watch the fireworks wore coats and hats and laid out blankets in the backs of their trucks. Thad almost didn't go. His arm, still in a cast, hurt on a spectrum from a dull throb to piercing agony, depending on the position he was in and the passage of time since his last OxyContin. The Fourth was the biggest social event of the year, and he didn't feel like talking to anyone—explaining again how he'd managed to break his arm so badly while fishing. But in the end he caved to tradition. He couldn't remember missing one in his whole life. As Thad and Hazen had grown older, their Fourth of July tradition had solidified. They and their father would head to the Blue Goose around four and have a few drinks.

After that they would all walk down to the rodeo grounds, where they bought a case of beer and divided the cans evenly in plastic grocery sacks topped with ice. Then, fully equipped, they would ascend the grandstand and take in the spectacle.

At a Fourth of July a few years before he died, they'd been in their usual seats enjoying the parade of jean-clad female forms passing them by, and Thad had asked their father why he had never dated or gotten married again. As a rule, their father did not discuss women, with them or anyone else as far as they knew. Some men avoid discussions of religion; some men tune out when things turn to sports, or cars, or hunting, or politics. For their father, it was women. Except for on the Fourth of July, which for some reason was the one time a year he would ever even acknowledge that there were these other members of the human race with certain characteristics that could be appealing in the right light. When Thad had asked him about remarriage, or at least going on a date, or even offering one of the big-haired full-figured ladies he was ogling a beer, he'd gone quiet. Thad thought maybe he'd offended him. It was a question he'd never thought to ask, and when he'd said it he immediately wished he hadn't. His father hadn't said anything. He'd finished his beer and crushed his can and they watched a bronc rider get thrown by a nasty crow-hopping paint. When the rodeo clown began to prattle on, his father had laughed and shook his head and fished out another beer. He said, "I came to this rodeo for the first time almost thirty years ago. I think this is the same damn rodeo clown. You'd think in that much time he'd have learned a new set of jokes. I mean, Jesus."

That was the end of that conversation, and Thad had never brought it up again. As far as he knew, his father had been faithful to their mother up until the day he died.

Lately, he'd wondered if his father's illness hadn't interrupted some sort of, if not planned, then generally agreed upon, course that would have eventually reunited him with Sacajawea. Thad and his mother still didn't talk much, but Thad had, one night at the kitchen sink, asked her if she would have come back and stayed if their father had still been alive.

She continued to rinse a green pureed glop out of the blender and then turned off the sink and began to towel the blender dry. Finally, after the thing was clean and put back on its stand, she said, "I remember when you were young, you used to like to skip stones. We'd go to that big pool on the river right above the bridge and you'd look for the perfect rock. Sometimes you'd find one so good, so flat and smooth, that you wouldn't even want to throw it. I always thought that was a funny thing. That you'd find something that was perfectly suited for exactly what you wanted to do, but something about that fact, that it was perfect, made you unable to actually do it."

She was wiping her hands dry with a dish towel, and when she was done she folded it and put it on the handle of the stove. Thad thought that was it, but then she continued. "When you skip rocks, sometimes they fly out straight and skip almost continuously, really close together on the water's surface, *bang, bang, bang,* like that. But sometimes you get ones that skip only once and then go really far in the air before plunking down. The two rocks have traveled the same distance. The end result is the same. Sometimes you get a rock that won't skip at all, just kerploosh, right there at your feet. See what I mean?"

Thad rolled his eyes, said he had no idea what she was talking about, and went out to rummage around in the gear shed.

In truth, he kind of knew what she was getting at.

One evening, August 15 only a week away, he told Sacajawea about the house.

"I guess you should know," he said. "Your folks built it, you were born in it, and now this."

Sacajawea asked him how much, and when he told her she sipped her tea, put her cup down precisely before responding. "I have some savings," she said.

How could someone like her have savings? *How?* That's what he wanted to say, what he couldn't wrap his head around. *How? How? How?* At least in this one capacity, gathering money, she had succeeded, somehow, in a way that seemed to elude him.

In the end, he called the accountant and Sacajawea paid the bill. The whole situation was cleared up in a day. How quickly a weight could be lifted from his shoulders, only to be immediately replaced by something more resembling a yoke. Thad hated the feeling of owing Sacajawea. But then, what man on earth isn't his mother's debtor? There could hardly be another way.

That fall, Thad quickly realized that running the saw would be impossible. Just lifting the heavy Stihl shot a marrow-deep pain through his forearm, and trying to apply force to run the blade through a log was unbearable. For a while Thad loaded and stacked and Hazen cut. This was not how it had ever been before. When they were young, their father ran the saw and they both carried armloads of cut firewood and slowly filled the truck bed. Mindless work, innumerable trips back and forth. Around age sixteen Thad started running the saw. Their father, at this point body broken from a lifetime of this, stayed home. Hazen did most of the loading, and that was how it had always been.

Cold mornings. Thad carried the battered green Stanley thermos that had been their father's. He gave Hazen plenty of direction on the proper use of the saw. Cut angles, the correct method for felling standing timber to ensure the blade didn't bind.

"Yeah," Hazen said. "I know." And it appeared that he did. He felled lodgepoles and bucked them up into neat, stove-sized rounds, and Thad drove the truck and loaded the pieces. Thad issued constant admonishments about safety. Hazen grunted and didn't cut himself. He ran the saw well. The morning grass was pewter, frost in the trees. The smoke and smell of the two-stroke gas burning hung low, and the snarl of the saw echoed from the hills.

When it got to the point where simply lifting a cut piece of wood made Thad grit his teeth, he went to the doctor. The break hadn't healed properly, and late that fall he went back in for surgery. At the hospital, his arm was re-broken, and a plate was installed with titanium screws.

FOR MOST OF THAT WINTER, THAD BARELY LEFT THE house. The pain was a problem, and there were pills for the pain, but then eventually the pills became the problem. Thad knew that this was the case, and he told himself that when spring came he'd be done with them. He'd already gotten a refill on his prescription and the doctor seemed a little surprised that he still needed them so regularly. But it was a bad break, after all. The doctor had told him that some people in his situation actually had to resort to amputation.

Sometimes he'd put on his boots and coat and hat and sit at the kitchen table finishing a cup of coffee as if readying for an errand. Sometimes he stepped out onto the porch and the snow crunching under his boots would grate his ears a certain way that made forward progress impossible. The days were short, and he slept for tremendous lengths of time. He half expected a knock at the door, the cops or the FWP coming with some kind of damning evidence, a bag of bear gallbladders with their fingerprints on it. His rational mind knew it was unlikely at this point, but still—a dull background dread cast his days.

Sacajawea was working days bagging groceries and stocking shelves at the hippy health food store in town. In the seventies a new age cult had bought up a bunch of land west of the river. They built a church with a giant gold pyramid spire, and there were rumors of bomb shelters up in the hills. The people seemed harmless enough. They wore purple and ate vegetarian. Some said they were stockpiling weapons. According to their prophetess founder, the world was set to descend into anarchy on a certain date, and when that date came and went without Armageddon, most of the followers moved on, or stayed and wound their way, sheepishly, into the fabric of the town. Several of them pooled their money and started the health food store. They had bulk food bins. Three large walls of supplements. There were shelves of organic produce, always on the verge of spoiling, so the place had a certain moldering air. Thad supposed it was a perfect fit for Sacajawea.

Hazen had gotten her van up and running.

Sometimes Thad got out their father's old fly-tying kit and sat with it at the table near the woodstove. He'd never become a good fly tier, never had the patience to sit and learn much beyond the basics. He tried to replicate the spruce flies and muddlers their father had preferred to use in the fall for brown trout. Hazen would occasionally wander in from wherever he'd been, face wind-chapped, nose running, and pick up Thad's most recent creation, holding it up to the light coming through the window. "Might work," he'd say.

His arm hurt, and just holding the bobbin or scissors at a certain angle was enough to send him back to the couch or his bed with the curtains drawn against whatever weak light the winter sun was throwing that day.

Sometime in midwinter, Thad started noticing a particularly foul smell wafting from Hazen in the few moments a day they spent in each other's proximity. To Thad, the days had long taken on a sort of blurred patina of sleep and stupor on the couch. Occasionally Hazen would pass through the living room or kitchen, and an acrid, musky stink would linger in his wake until Thad finally asked him if something had died in his boots.

Hazen was standing at the sink in the kitchen eating a sandwich, mustard dripping down his fingers. He sniffed his jacket sleeve, chewed and swallowed, took another big bite, and shrugged. "I guess mink don't smell too good," he said around a mouthful of ham and cheese. Thad waited for him to elaborate, but he kept on eating. Looking out the window, occasionally stopping to lick the mustard from his wrist.

"What are you doing with mink?" Thad said finally.

"I got a job," Hazen said. "The guy down on Mill Creek that runs those dogsled tours? I'm working for him."

"You're dogsledding?"

"I'm taking care of the dogs. I feed them twice a day. Clean the straw out of their houses. Shovel up the shit. Fifty-three dogs. Lots of shit."

"What does this have to do with mink?"

"I feed them mink."

"You're feeding mink? The dogsled guy has mink too?"

"No. I feed them mink. The dogs. They eat mink. My boss has a deal with a mink farmer over in Gallatin Gateway. They raise the mink, kill them, and skin them, and then they have all these dead mink. My boss goes over and gets them and freezes them in a big chest freezer at his place, and then when they're solid as a rock I cut them into pieces with a band saw. Then I feed them to the dogs. Kind of like little mink nuggets. They love them. Lots of fat and oil in a mink, my boss says. Good food for dogs."

"Jesus Christ," Thad said. "How'd you get in with this guy?"

"He was advertising a Subaru for sale. Had a sign for it up on the board at Coffee Crossings. A 1985 Legacy. Low miles."

"You were thinking of buying this guy's ancient Subaru?"

"I don't really have any money. But I called the guy and went over to look at it. He wanted twenty-five hundred for it. Runs good. I told him I didn't have any money. And he told me he needed someone to help out with the dogs, and so we made a deal. Next month he gives me the Subaru, and if I want to keep working there, I can, but he'll start paying me. But if I don't want to keep working there, I don't have to and I still get the car. Pretty good deal, I thought."

This conversation was making Thad's head hurt. It might actually have been a good deal. It was hard to say. At some previous time Thad knew he would have had a more clear opinion on it. "Did you sign a contract?" Thad said.

"Nah, we shook hands."

Thad was starting to head back to the couch. "You better hope he doesn't burn you," he said over his shoulder. "You should've gotten something in writing."

"He won't burn me," Hazen said. "He's an all right guy."

"Everyone's an all right guy, until they're not," Thad said, stretching out with his damaged arm elevated on a pillow the way the doctors said to do.

Hazen went out, and the noxious blend of dog shit and mink wafted after him. "Leave those clothes on the porch before you come in here again," Thad shouted at the sound of him heading down the porch. "And wash your goddamn ass."

EARLY SPRING. MUD AND DEAD GRASS. THE SNOW COM-ing off and occasional warm blasts of wind coming down from the northwest. Bears went to bed for the winter, and so had Thad. With the cast off, Thad's arm looked pale yellow and misshapen, a noticeable divot and a long scar from the surgery. He puttered around the house and yard. Simple tasks, like picking up fallen cottonwood branches, left him tired and reeling. He made pots of coffee, pouring a cup, forgetting until it had gone cold, then pouring another. He had a small mountain of poorly tied flies in a jumble on the desk.

"We should go fishing," Hazen said.

"Too cold," Thad said.

"The fish don't care," Hazen said.

"Too cold for me," Thad said. In truth, he wasn't sure if he could cast. His arm still hurt. It had gotten to the point where he couldn't tell if it was in his head or not. He'd think about performing some action, unscrewing a tight lid on the peanut butter jar, for instance, and he'd start it like normal and then feel the twinge shoot up his right arm, and then he'd switch, unscrew the lid with the left. Sometimes he thought that he could feel the pain before he even started the action itself, and then he wondered if the source of the pain was somewhere in his brain, if the pain had become some sort of bad habit, like lying around, like the pills, and then he'd tell himself to snap out of it and go do something in the yard for a half an hour. Then he'd get exhausted, sleep on the couch for the rest of the afternoon.

He felt soft, overall. Which was a new experience in his life. A sponginess to his midsection and arms that seemed to penetrate straight through to the very core. Sometimes he went out to the gear shed and moved things around. There was the eight-pound splitting maul that he'd swung without too much effort for countless hours in the past. Now, just lifting it to move it from one corner to the other seemed like a great strain. And his arm hurt.

Sacajawea brought him things from the hippy food store. Amino acid supplements. Essential oils. Loose-leaf yerba maté teas. CBD balms and lotions. He rolled his eyes at her and left them on the kitchen table. Sometimes he rubbed the CBD balm on his arm when no one was home. It made no discernible difference. The supplements elicited strange-smelling belches. The tea tasted like water infused with dusty hay. He told himself that spring was coming and that was going to make all the difference. He told himself that when the sun reached the right angle in the afternoons, he was going to emerge, skinny and weak but ravenous. Dangerous.

Hazen came home with his Subaru. It was low-slung, the old boxy body style, dull silver with a mismatched burgundy door, replaced from a salvage yard. Thad walked around the car with his hands in his pockets. "Not much rust," he said.

"Nope," Hazen said. "Fires right up every time."

Thad kicked a tire. "Good tread left."

"Yep," Hazen said. "New last year."

"Definitely old enough for the permanent plates. You going to get insurance?"

"I'm not sure. Maybe. I just got it; haven't figured out that far ahead yet."

"Let me know if you need help."

"Will do."

Hazen was leaning against the fender. He sniffed and spit. Thad could smell the mink on him. "Guess who I saw yesterday?" Hazen said.

Thad shrugged.

"I went in County Market for a sandwich and saw the Scot in there. He was pushing around a cart full of food. Like he was really stocking up. He told me to tell you hi."

Thad hadn't put on a jacket and the cold was getting to him. He hunched his shoulders and pushed his hands deeper into his pockets. "What else did he say?"

"He just said to say hi. Said he might swing by sometime for a chat."

"A chat."

"That's what he said."

"OK." Thad suppressed a shiver. "I'm surprised. Didn't think he'd show his face around here again."

Hazen laughed. "I'm not surprised," he said.

"Why's that?"

"Didn't feel finished."

"What's that supposed to mean? What's finished feel like?"

"Guess that depends. His daughter was with him."

"Yeah?"

"She told me howdy."

"She actually said that to you? 'Howdy, Hazen'?"

"She just said howdy. That's it. I'm not sure she remembers my name. She seems real nice though. I don't think she likes being up there with him."

"What do you mean?"

"She looked at me."

"Looked at you?"

"Yeah. Like she wanted to tell me something." Hazen widened his eyes and leaned in. "She did this with her eyes, you know? I don't think she's happy. I've heard some stuff. People are saying the Scot got busted because of that kid he shot. The kid's mom hired a private investigator to follow the Scot around. They got photos of him doing something. Then the Scot pled guilty and got a deal and now he's back, and people are saying that he came back to get even with the kid's mom. For turning him in."

Hazen shrugged and leaned against the car.

"Don't be talking to those people. And don't be going to the Goose."

"I know." Hazen gave a dismissive wave of his hand and rubbed at a spot of something on the Subaru's hood. Thad watched him. At a point not too long in the past he wouldn't have let it rest here. He didn't like that little dismissive wave. He knew he should press the point. Hazen needed occasional checking. It had been that way since they were kids. If you let him get going on his own lead, he was liable to do something stupid.

"Watch yourself, pal," Thad said. But there wasn't anything behind it. It was hollow. Hazen didn't even look up from what he was doing.

"Sure, man," he said. "I heard you." He spit on the Subaru's hood and rubbed ferociously with his jacket elbow. Thad went inside and lay down.

THAD SAT ON THE PORCH AND SLIT AN ENVELOPE OPEN with his pocketknife. He had the little .22 pistol in his coat pocket that their father had used to shoot at magpies. He'd been sitting waiting like that on the porch for several afternoons. The days were nice, and he could hear the river as he walked down the long drive to get the mail. After the resolution of the tax lien situation, he'd resurrected the mailbox. The hospital bills he still put in the woodstove unopened. Electric, gas, and phone he stacked with the others on the kitchen table. On this particular day there was a letter addressed to him, handwritten, with a return address and name he didn't recognize.

From the envelope, Thad removed a neatly penned letter on thick, creamy unlined paper. Some kind of corporate letterhead, a generic name, Anderson Logistics, Seattle, Washington. Thad knew what it was the minute he read the first sentence:

"I've recently bought a section of land adjacent to yours, and I wondered if you'd be interested . . . ." Thad stopped reading and scanned for an amount. It was there, and it was a staggering sum. He had the letter in his hand and instead of crumpling it and tossing it in the fire the way he had always done before, and his father had always done before that, he folded it and slipped it in his pocket.

The doctor refused him another refill. After Thad had the last pill, he knew it wasn't going to be good, but he was surprised by just how bad it actually was. He'd had the flu only once in his early teens. He'd been bedridden for two weeks, couldn't keep anything down, sweating through his sheets every night until morning, at which point he'd start shivering. This was like that, but with a sharper edge. The noise of his brother entering the house and slamming his boots off in the mudroom sent piercing shards through his brain. He was exhausted but couldn't actually fall asleep for any length of time. He couldn't eat. The roots of his hair ached. He lay on the couch and watched whatever was on. They didn't have cable. *Wheel of Fortune* was on in the afternoons, *Jeopardy!* after that.

He no longer had it in him to roll his eyes or scoff at the offerings made to him by Sacajawea. She arranged crystals on the coffee table, close enough for him to reach. She put a pink Himalayan salt lamp on an end table next to the couch, and its soft glow lent a florid cast to his already-fevered dreams. She brought him detoxifying charcoal tablets. Probiotic kombucha tonics. She heated him cups of bone broth, which was the only thing he could keep down. He felt himself draining in some elemental way, hollowing day by day. He occasionally had the thought that it could go one of two ways. Either he'd empty until there was nothing left and a strong wind would blow him away, or he'd slowly fill back up, and what he'd been before would be replaced with something different altogether. He'd heard somewhere that every ten years the cells in your body are completely renewed. He felt that it was happening to him now in some sort of accelerated process that he wasn't sure he'd survive.

One night Sacajawea came and sat cross-legged on the floor in front of the couch and spoke to him in the way she had when they were kids. She lit sage and blew on the glowing embers to make the smoke thick. She told him a story in which she was the main character.

"IN THE SUMMER OF MY NINETEENTH YEAR, I STILL RODE my childhood horse everywhere. It was a big bay gelding that had been old ten years before. The other girls in my class had gone on to jobs, marriages, college even. I had started wrapping myself in my quilt and sitting on the porch, spending almost no time thinking about my future. Already I had trouble sleeping. I'd go barefoot across the wood floors and out the door into darkness and go to stand at the corral, whistling for my horse. The horse was surefooted in the dark, and I'd grab a handful of its mane and swing up, lean down to open the gate, and then let the horse go where it pleased. Sometimes we wandered down to the river and the horse would drink and I would feel the rise and fall of its sides like a bellows between my bare thighs.

"What happened was my mother and father went on an overnight trip to Kooskia, Idaho, to see about the purchase of a mare. On the way back they hit a late-winter storm coming down the backside of Lolo Pass. There was a head-on collision with a logging truck. My father had purchased the horse, and it was in the trailer when it happened, and although both my parents died, the horse apparently survived. When someone came upon the scene of the accident, the horse trailer was tilted on its side but empty. The wind had obscured any tracks in the snow and the horse had disappeared.

"A week later I drove my mother's car to the scene of the accident. I parked at the rest stop overlook on the pass and went and stood at the edge of the road where there were small pieces of broken radiator and taillight scattered over the snow. I looked up and down the road. I looked onto the plow-thrown drift and the plunge down the slope. No cars passed, and I remember wishing one would. I wanted someone to see me. Maybe they would stop and tell me not to do it. I waited and no one came, and then I tightened the straps on my pack and climbed over the guardrail.

"I searched for nearly a month. I was constantly wet, and several times I thought I was going to freeze to death. The rivers were huge and violent. Their tributaries fell short and hard down rocky impassable canyons. I slipped crossing one of these and was carried downstream, bouncing off rocks, nearly getting entangled in a downed tree. I finally ended up on a small gravel beach and I lay there thinking that, if I moved, I'd find that my bones were broken and splintered, my insides pulped like fruit. When my clothing started to freeze and stiffen on my body, I knew that if I didn't move I would die, so I dragged myself up to the trees and gathered handfuls of dry witch's hair and started a fire.

"Of the mare I saw little sign. Tracks at the edge of the river smeared and overlaid with the small cloven prints of deer. Places where the snow had been pawed through by hoofs to expose the winter-bleached grass below. On several occasions I saw strands of tail or mane strung on low-hanging branches, and I felt like I was closing in. Once, I came across a bird's nest jammed in the crotch of an aspen, its interior lined with long coarse filaments of pale-gray hair. I looked at this for a long time; then I pulled it from the tree and kicked it apart.

"Occasionally I'd hear sounds like the clopping of unshod hooves on rock, and I'd run to a high point or climb a tree to scan the area. I imagined the horse was reverting back to some ancestral state, its coat un-curried and thick, walking between the trees, tangle-maned, going walleyed at the sight of man.

"The horse eluded me in waking moments and then made itself willfully domestic in dreams. It came to me and snuffled oats from my hand. I led it from pasture to barn and stood in a warm stall running the curry comb over its flanks until its coat sparked and shone. Sometimes my father would come out and nod as if appreciative of the work I was doing.

"The food I'd brought lasted a week, and after that I survived on whatever I could find. I ate the moss off trees. When I came across the carcasses of animals, I picked through for whatever scraps the other scavengers had left. Once I found a dead cow elk reduced by coyotes to not much more than hide and hoof and bone. I gathered up what I could and made a fire. I used a rock to pound the bones into small pieces that would fit in my aluminum pan. I covered the bone pieces with snow and boiled it for a long time, until the bones became soft, and then I strained them away and drank the broth.

"As late winter moved on to spring, my boots began to rot off my feet and the tips of my hair took on a tinge of green. The snow was gone for the most part, and ferns began to poke up through the humus. I ate the fiddleheads and wandered through a green and dripping world. Everything smelled like skunk. I thought of my parents. I obsessed myself with the specifics, all the violent details. Would their bodies have been recognizable to me? Had their passing been instantaneous? Maybe my father had come awake briefly, upside down in the blood-glazed truck cab. Had he looked out the broken windshield and thought the world itself fractured? Had my mother screamed? Had their blood soaked into the earth, or had some of it been carried with the melting snow? And if it flowed, how long before it eventually found its way into the Pacific? How long before it came back down to me in rain?

"At first I thought that I could sense the horse's presence in the country. Stale hoofprints, hardened droppings in the alder thickets. Occasionally I'd enter a small canyon and the air would be filled with the unmistakable smell of horse. Gradually these occurrences became less and less frequent. I'd cast a line to this horse, tethered myself to it as a way of anchoring myself to the world, but as the horse continued to escape me, I felt my own connection to things slipping.

"In all this time I was comfortable only once. I came across a hot spring that flowed down a rock face covered with a sheet of electric-green algae. I got in and wriggled down into the rank sulfur mud and leaned back so just my nose and mouth and eyes were above waterline. I lay perfectly still, staring at the sky. Tall ponderosa pines framed the pool. I couldn't see sunsets or sunrises, just the color change in the clouds on the periphery. While I was submerged in the pool I saw strange things. A flock of starlings descended in a crowd to cover the ground around me. They washed themselves in the shallow water and left their tracks in the mud. I thought their tracks were a kind of message. A cuneiform I was unable to read. At one point a coyote came to the edge of the water. Its coat was patchy with mange. It wouldn't look me in the eyes, and it left with my stained and ripped wool sweater in its mouth. I remember inventing constellations from the stars that swirled in my section of sky. Odd shapes: wheelbarrows, bicycles, locomotives on celestial tracks, the Milky Way like a smoke plume rising from its stack. Sometimes, no sooner had I traced the outline of a figure in my mind than the whole thing would dissolve in a shower of meteor, leaving something new and altogether different in its place.

"I felt myself softening. My bones became spongy and waterlogged. I had settled so completely into the muck I wasn't sure I'd be able to break free. I hadn't eaten in days. When I ran my fingers through my hair, clumps of it came loose and wafted through the water. I knew that if I didn't leave that place soon, I was going to die. I could picture how it would go. For a while my body would pollute the pool, and then the worms and the insects would break me down until I was just a brilliant white skeleton, and then even that would settle and disappear."

"I eventually emerged from the water and stumbled into my clothing. Because the sweater was gone, I wrapped myself in my wet bedroll and set out shuffling, taking whatever path was easiest. I knew the horse was gone and that my inability to find the animal had doomed me in a way that seemed utterly complete and final.

"When I staggered into the logger's camp, I hadn't seen another person in weeks. The air smelled like cut pine and burning diesel. There was a plastic milk jug with the top cut off full of bacon grease, hardened and waxy in the cold. I scooped handfuls of it into my mouth, retching almost immediately. And that's how he found me. He wrapped me in a wool blanket and carried me into the cook tent. I could hear chainsaws somewhere in the distance. Men shouting. I fell asleep thinking that there was a good chance that someone here, at this very camp, had been behind the wheel of the truck that killed my parents.

"I stayed there for a couple days. The logger who found me was kind, and he told me he'd give me a ride home on Sunday. When the day came, I rode with him, and although he didn't ask I told him the whole story. Eventually I fell asleep and didn't wake up until hours later, when he needed my help to find the right driveway.

"He'd planned on dropping me off and then immediately turning around for the four-hour drive back to camp. I told him I'd make him coffee for the road and brought him inside. It was cold and musty in the house, so he lit a fire in the woodstove and left the door open so the smell of burning pine would clean the air. I made him the coffee and we sat next to the woodstove. He was on the couch and I was on the rug. When he started to leave, I put myself on his lap. He said he had to go in the morning, but he never did. He never quite got around to it.

"Months later we went to the Fourth of July rodeo together. I wore a loose skirt and cowboy boots, and he wore a paisley silk scarf around his neck and new blue jeans that made his legs look like stovepipes. We sat close together on the bleachers in the grandstands, and when it grew dark and the fireworks exploded out over the river and lit up the Beartooths, he proposed. I didn't know for sure but thought I might be pregnant. I said yes, obviously. He was thirty-seven and I was only nineteen. I felt older."

During the telling Sacajawea had reached out and put her hand on his arm, and for some reason Thad couldn't force himself to move it away. A deep lethargy had settled in him. Sage smoke in his eyes. Sacajawea waved the smoldering bundle around his head.

"Did your father ever tell you about the first time I left? It was when you two were really young. I don't know if you remember.

"Your father broke his hand in the woods. He couldn't work for months. I hadn't had a job since you were born, but all of a sudden, we had nothing coming in. I had a girlfriend who worked in the park in the summer, then went to Northern California to work in Humboldt for the winter. She told me about it. She said it wasn't too hard of a job, tedious, you sat in a room and trimmed the buds and listened to music and chatted with the other girls. They always hired girls to do the trimming,

I learned that later. It killed me to leave you two that first time. I put you to bed. I remember you fighting it, trying not to sleep. I think you knew something was happening. You were always very aware of your surroundings, even when you were tiny. You finally fell asleep and my friend came to pick me up, and I cried for the first two hours of our drive. It's a funny thing, at the time being a mother of two and still being naive about so many things. You'd think that the state of motherhood would come with a certain understanding of the world and your place in it. But it doesn't. It doesn't. Motherhood conveys responsibility. It conveys a certain ache. It doesn't grant knowledge. For a long time, I thought this was a flaw in the makeup of the world itself. How can the universe create this class of being, a mother, and not grant that being the tools necessary to successfully fulfill her role? It seems like an impossibility, evolutionarily speaking.

"I got out there and it was OK for a while. I learned how to do the work. It really wasn't too hard, and the cash came at the end of every week. We all lived in this trailer way back up in the redwoods. I remember the first time the fog came in. I went out to the porch at night, and the fog came through the trees like it was alive, a gray mystical thing. It was a long time ago, but I'm trying to tell you how it was. At first, we just worked and made big dinners and only drank wine. Family dinners we called them, although every time I said that I felt a pang, because I knew I had an actual family and these people weren't it. It was fun for a while, and then it wasn't. They hired girls to do the trimming for a reason, and eventually things started happening. There were altered states of consciousness, and I did things and things were done to me. I could have left. I mean, no one physically restrained me there. And I thought about it a lot. I could hitch out to the road. Catch a bus. Be back home with you and your brother. And for a while I told myself I wasn't going to do that because we needed the money. I was there for the money, and I was going to see it through, and then at some point I knew that I wasn't leaving because I was unfit to return here. Deep in my core, unfit to be a mother and a wife. Does that make sense? There was guilt and there was shame. And I was young too. I can't deny that. I'd seen so little. It got to the point that I felt that if I was already tarnished, then I was going to enjoy whatever mean pleasure being tarnished gained you. I was a mother of two and I thought I needed to learn what it meant to be a woman. I remember crying the first time I saw the ocean. I jumped in, and it was so much colder than I imagined it would be.

"Eventually your father came and got me. I told him I wasn't coming back. He dragged me out of the trailer, and when one of the men there tried to stop him your father punched him in the throat with the hand that still wore the cast, and the man dropped like he'd been killed. I'd never seen your father act violently before. He threw me in his truck, and I was crying, saying vile things, saying I would rather die than go back with him. I don't know why I was saying these things because I didn't mean them, not really, but for some reason I thought it would be easier to live with myself if I knew he no longer wanted me. He threw me in the truck and he drove, and at one point he put his hand around my throat, and he had this look in his eye, and I thought he was going to choke me to death right there. But he didn't, and I cried until I fell asleep, and he drove straight through the night. I'd left everything I'd come with. I didn't even get most of the money I was owed. Your father took the cast off his hand and he went back to the woods. Whatever else I could say about him, all the man knew and felt comfortable with was work. That night, when he grabbed me by the neck like that, I cried out. He let me go, and that was the last time he ever touched me with anything approaching warmth. He hardly ever touched me again."

Sacajawea patted Thad's thigh. "I'm sorry; maybe this is more than you want to hear."

THE KNOCKING CAME AT MIDDAY. IT INTRUDED ON A woman in a floral muumuu spinning the Wheel of Fortune. Thad, on the couch, felt that his destiny, such as it was, spun before him. Every stop on the wheel read BANKRUPT. The knocking wouldn't stop, and he dragged himself up. Cheers from the TV, the beautiful white-sand beaches of Sandals Resort, Jamaica. The Scot was at the door, and Thad couldn't even remember what he'd done with the .22. He hadn't seen it in days. He looked down at himself. He was wearing stained sweatpants, a grimy old Park High Rangers sweatshirt. He put the hood up, some thin protective layer between his ears and the world, and stepped out.

He collapsed into a chair, and the Scot leaned against the porch rail looking at him. Thad could see his daughter behind the windshield of the Suburban. She was in the driver's seat for some reason Thad couldn't fathom. The light was dull and gray, but it seemed brutal and intense and Thad shaded his eyes. The Scot was a large silhouette in front of him.

"Seems like spring has finally sprung," the Scot said finally. "What a day."

"Nice," Thad said. He hadn't ventured outside yesterday. Things were greening up. It happened fast.

"Did I wake you up from a nap?"

"Under the weather. Been sick."

"Sorry to hear that."

Thad rubbed his face with his hands. He'd never been able to grow a full beard; it came in patchy, and so he usually shaved regularly. He hadn't in a while, and he knew how he must look. He'd caught his reflection in the bathroom mirror and his eyes were sunken pits, hair lank, a grayish cast to his skin. He wanted to be back on the couch. "What do you want?" he said.

The Scot looked toward the Suburban. "We were headed into town, and I thought we'd just pull in here to see how you were doing. I'd heard you weren't feeling well."

"Stop the bullshit," Thad said. "My head hurts." He raised his arm and pulled his sleeve down. His arm looked frail. His fingers thin and pale as birch twigs. The long scar and depression in the flesh of his forearm was stark in the light. "My arm is fucked. Why'd you come back? I never thought I'd see you around here again."

"My home is here," the Scot said. "Why would I not be back? I had a few things I needed to take care of back East, family matters, and now we're back, and this is where we'll be."

"What do you want?"

"It's unfortunate about your arm, but we had a deal," the Scot said. "I invested in you boys and had no return. That's where we're at right now."

"You called us in. I know it was you. There was no other way. They knew we were out there because you turned over, and that's why you left. I'm past it. I've got other problems. You want your money back? Get in line, pal. Right after the hospital and everyone else that's after me. You want my advice? Go back to whatever shithole you came from. Ohio, or wherever it is. I'm not hung up on it, but some of those other guys might be. If I were you I'd be looking over my shoulder."

The Scot laughed and pointed at Thad, who was starting to rise. "Sit your ass down, son."

Thad sat. If he'd had a gun he would have shot him right there. He would have. He spit on the porch somewhere close to the Scot's hairy red leg.

"Not your son," he said.

The Scot waved this away and sighed. "You don't know anything," he said. "You don't even know how much you don't know. There's more people involved in this. You think I rolled you over? I got rolled over on."

"Your name was never in the paper. You got a deal."

"The American justice system is not a level playing field. I will admit that. My lawyer is a good lawyer. He is not a cheap lawyer. And so my name wasn't in the paper. As far as I can tell, you two got out of this as well as anyone. Better than most. So I really don't understand the hard feelings."

"I don't have any money."

The Scot crossed his legs and smoothed his kilt. "I'm not surprised. Winter. Medical bills. All that. I bet you're getting anxious to get back up in there and retrieve what you stashed."

During this whole conversation, Thad had felt like he was one step behind, groping through a fog, but now there was a clearing and he understood. He laughed. "You think we stashed those things? I was passed out in the bottom of a raft hemorrhaging blood. Hazen, for once, showed some good sense and pitched them over before we came under the bridge. Get yourself a mask and snorkel. I bet there's still a few stuck to the bottom up there."

"A mask and a snorkel," the Scot said. He looked back over his shoulder toward the Suburban and gave his daughter a wave. "You haven't been to town much this winter, have you? You two have become quite the folk heroes. Ran the canyons and stashed the goods. *Outlaws.* They'll be singing ballads about you before long."

"We didn't stash anything."

"And that's not all. There's some people saying that you found something up there. A valuable something. That you're just biding your time until you can go back and get it."

"What are you even talking about? We had a decent load of antlers that we scrounged around all over the damn place to get. We tossed them in the river. End of story."

"The park is a mysterious place," the Scot said. "I don't need to tell you that. Geological oddities, early human inhabitation, the remains of extinct animals. I've read up on it. Did you know that they've found the skulls of ancient rhinoceroses in the park? Mammoth tusks. And gold, of course."

"Rhinoceroses? You're insane."

"Maybe. Maybe not. Where is your brother?"

"I don't know. At work probably."

"You realize that he's not as tight-lipped as you? He's been in the Goose this winter. Talking about things."

"Hazen is saying that we found a rhinoceros?"

"Don't get hung up on the rhinoceros. That was just an example. He's saying that you found a lot of antlers. And maybe something else. A valuable something else. And it's all stashed in a safe place. And so when this comes back to me, you can see how I might be a little perturbed. As your investor."

"He's full of shit. Especially if he's been drinking at the Goose. He'd say anything if he thought people wanted to hear it."

The Scot straightened up and started down the porch steps. Halfway down he stopped. He spoke, looking out down the driveway and the steep pitch of the mountains behind that. "Me, you, and Hazen will have a meeting and get this straightened out," he said. "I'd suggest you talk to him. I'll see you later."

Thad rose from the chair and went inside. He looked for the .22 and couldn't find it. He looked under the couch, and while he was there he lay down. His arm throbbed and he held it to his chest. He thought he'd probably be willing to cut if off himself for one more bottle of those pills. No pain, easy sleep.

THEY WERE GOING TO TOWN IN HAZEN'S SUBARU. THAD was riding shotgun. It smelled like dog. Rotting mink. Thad rolled the window down and Hazen fiddled with the radio until he found something he liked—pop country, the more star-spangled and chicken-fried the better. Stupid music made by smart people to make money off stupid people. Thad hated it. "It's just music," Hazen said. "Who cares?"

They were going to town so that Thad could help Hazen get the Subaru licensed and registered at the county building. Hazen was nervous about doing it by himself and had asked Thad sheepishly, kicking one boot against another in the kitchen.

"Guess I don't have much else going on," Thad said. "Let me get dressed."

It had been a week since the Scot showed up, and Thad hadn't said anything to Hazen. He'd barely seen him. These days Hazen was gone shortly after dawn and didn't return until long after Thad was asleep. They were heading up the river road and Thad was watching Hazen drive. Normally Thad drove everywhere, and now he was riding shotgun, looking for something to criticize. Thad couldn't remember Hazen ever taking driver's ed. Probably he had; Thad just couldn't remember it happening. Hazen drove just fine, and Thad lowered the window more, the rush of air doing something to blunt the dumb sounds pouring out of the Subaru's speakers. There were elk feeding under the pivot in the Anderson's hay field, and Hazen slowed slightly. The animals had the patchy, moth-eaten look of spring. Hazen sped up again, hammering the Subaru a little so Thad could hear the engine. It sounded OK, Thad thought. For a twenty-year-old station wagon.

"Have you seen that pistol around?" Thad said.

"Huh?"

Thad turned the stereo down and rolled his window up slightly, even though he knew Hazen had heard him just fine. "Dad's magpie gun. I can't find it," he said.

Hazen shrugged. "I have it," he said.

"Why?"

Hazen was squinting into the sun, sitting ramrod straight, hands ten and two on the wheel. "Had to put a dog down," he said. "Fifty-four dogs, and sometimes you have to put one down. It happens. They're not pets, you know?"

"Why doesn't the guy you work for put down his own dogs? Why does he have you doing it?"

"It's hard for him. They're a little more like pets to him. I'm not as attached, I guess. They're not my dogs. He doesn't have a gun, either."

"I think a man should put down his own dogs, if he has to. That's all I'm saying. Doesn't seem right."

"He gave me an extra fifty to do it. I don't like doing it. But it's not the worst thing. Not like having to put down a pet, because they're not pets."

"See? He pays you more out of guilt. He knows it's his responsibility. Next time you should ask him for a hundred."

"Yeah?" Hazen said. "I don't know about that. No one likes to kill a dog. It's just one of those things."

At the county building, Thad ushered Hazen through the DMV and the county treasurer. After some deliberation, Hazen picked out the classic blue Montana license plate with the outline of the state. "I didn't realize there'd be so many options," he said.

When they emerged, Hazen was holding his paperwork and license plates, smiling so big that Thad had to laugh and shake his head.

"All right," he said. "I'll buy you a beer to celebrate."

They headed to the Goose, and to Thad's surprise, Hazen insisted on buying, a first as far as he could remember. "I'm making decent money," Hazen said. "And If I come back next winter, I'll get a raise."

They had their beer and Hazen put down his cash with a flourish, and when they emerged from the dim bar, blinking in the late-afternoon sun, the Scot was leaning against the Subaru. This time, he was by himself.

THERE WERE ACCUSATIONS. VEHEMENT DENIALS FROM Hazen. At one point the Scot grabbed Thad's bad arm as he attempted to brush by him and open the Subaru door. The Scot's big hairy fingers gripped viselike around the metal plate in Thad's forearm. He let out a pained grunt and nearly buckled. Then Hazen rushed the Scot, swinging wildly. Hazen got in one glancing blow before the Scot pushed him to the ground and casually kicked him in the stomach before he could get up.

Hazen puked and was gasping on the sidewalk, and the Scot had his finger in Thad's face, saying something that Thad could barely hear over the thumping in his ears. The Scot walked off, smoothing the kilt along his thighs, and Thad heard his Suburban fire up and drive away.

Thad helped Hazen up and loaded him in the passenger seat of the Subaru. He had to drive home with his left hand. His right arm felt white-hot and he held it in his lap.

They sat in the car in the driveway.

"This is what happens when you run your mouth in the bar," Thad said. "Now people are believing all sorts of shit."

Thad was saying these things because he felt that he had to. More habit than anything else. He was having a hard time truly caring one way or another. He wanted to go lie down on the couch and sleep.

Hazen said nothing, then rolled his window down and spit. Eventually, he said, "When it comes right down to it, I might not have thrown all the antlers in the river."

"What's that?"

"I threw some of them in the river, but one raft I stashed up there. You were passed out. I didn't know if you were going to be pissed at me if I tossed them all. I thought I should just pitch them all in the river, but then I thought you'd be mad so I stashed half of them."

"Were you planning on telling me?"

Hazen smiled and pressed his stomach gingerly. "I was going to surprise you. I was waiting until you were feeling better. Then we could both go up and bring them out."

"Jesus Christ."

"What about this other stuff, telling people we found something else?"

Hazen laughed. "That was kind of like my hopes for the future, you know? There's all sorts of stuff in the park. There's really no telling what we could get. I was getting excited thinking about it."

"You realize what people have been saying? Why the Scot is so fired up? They think we have something, or know where something valuable is. Gold, or dinosaur bones, or some crazy shit. This isn't going to stop now. The more we deny, the more they think we're hiding something."

"A dinosaur bone?"

"I have no idea."

"If you want, I can just tell the Scot everything. I'll tell him I stashed some antlers but that's it. We can get the antlers for him, probably. I'm sure they're still there."

"We're not getting anything for the Scot. We're staying the hell away from him. We're going to let things calm down. We'll go to the cops if we have to."

"There was no reason for him to kick me like that."

"You're okay."

"I know."

"I need to go lie down. We'll figure something out. Don't be hanging out in town. Hear me?"

"Sure."

Thad got out of the car and stood for a few moments looking at the house. He could smell the river behind it, the cottonwood buds getting ready to pop. Ever since getting that letter, he'd had that astronomical figure in his head, not even letting himself dwell on it but just feeling its presence. The house and everything that needed doing. The roof. The road could use a grading. In the next year or two, he was going to have to re-chink the place, a long, tedious job. The hospital bills were like some sort of foul mist over everything he saw.

Hazen groaned when he straightened from the car. He held his stomach and spit. "Can't believe that asshole kicked me like that," he said.

"You're fine," Thad said.

Thad started walking to the house, and when he'd almost reached the steps, Hazen said, "Hey, Thad."

Thad turned to look at him. Hazen was leaning against the Subaru. His hair was loose and hung messy in his eyes, and he had a pale line of puke running down his sweatshirt. He spit again and looked off behind Thad at the cottonwoods that hid the river. "That guy I work for shoots his own dogs, if he needs to," Hazen said. "I just wanted to let you know that. He doesn't make me kill any dogs. I made that up. I took that .22 because I saw you had it next to you on the couch. I thought you were going to use it someday. You know what I mean? So I took it."

"Oh hell. It's not like that," Thad said. "That's not what it was about."

"OK, I just didn't know."

"I'm fine. You don't need to worry about me."

Hazen tucked some of his hair behind his ears. He stood up straighter. "You don't need to worry about me neither," he said. He laughed and thumped the hood of the Subaru. "Got ol' trusty now. Unstoppable. It'll be summer before you know it." He gave the goofy double thumbs-up he sometimes gave when he was really happy, and Thad shook his head and went inside to lie down.

Later Thad would replay this conversation in his memory, running it back and forth, scrutinizing it for anything that would shed light on what happened. There was nothing there. It was inscrutable. He sometimes wished he had a picture of his brother, standing there in front of his first car. Grinning like an idiot, double-thumbs-up happy, with puke on his shirt.

IT WAS SACAJAWEA WHO TOLD HIM. SHE CAME HOME from her shift at the hippy food store with a paper bag full of produce that was getting too past its prime to sell. She blended most of the stuff up for her smoothies. She always offered some to Thad if he was around. Some of her concoctions weren't that great: the sweet potato, kale, mango, and coconut was a real gagger. He did like her carrot ginger, surprisingly. Pretty sweet, kind of tangy. He and Sacajawea sometimes sat at the kitchen table and didn't say much. He no longer left rooms when she entered them. It was whatever it was. Life's too short, he told himself.

On that day she came home, and she started in with the blender. He was there in the kitchen, not doing much, just sitting there with that letter in his pocket. He was thinking of showing it to her. If he went that route, legally he didn't have to get her approval, but she'd been born in the house, and her father had made it with his bare hands, and she had saved it from the tax lien sale, after all.

She filled a large glass, and a smaller one with the leftovers, and put the smaller glass down in front of him. It was a deep red, beet-based maybe. He took a small sip. It was sort of bland. Not great, but not too offensive either. She sat down and held her smoothie, in both hands. Her lips were red-stained from the juice. "That guy with the kilt," she said. "They found him up at his place. A bear got him. I heard about it in the store today. Everyone in town is talking about it."

"A bear got him?" Thad said. "Like, *killed* him?" He put his smoothie down too quickly and it clunked on the tabletop.

"Yeah. Gruesome."

"Up at his house?"

"I guess the propane-truck-driver guy found him. He was up there to fill the tank, and he saw something weird and red off at the edge of the trees and it was his kilt. There he was, partially buried and, you know, he'd been *fed upon*."

"Was the bear still there?"

"I'm not sure. The propane guy called 911."

"Jesus Christ. Was his daughter up there?"

"I heard she's disappeared. But this is all just stuff I heard at the store. You know how it is. The guy telling me all this said a grizzly will sometimes bury its kill to keep other scavengers off it. I didn't know that."

Chunks of beet had risen to the top of the smoothie and it looked like a glass of congealing blood. "Have you see Hazen recently?" Thad said.

"Yesterday, I think," she said. "Maybe the day before that, actually. He mentioned something about going camping."

"Yeah? OK." Thad finished the smoothie in one big gulp. Too much too fast, and his stomach threatened to heave. He coughed and waited for it to settle before rinsing his glass. He headed out to rummage around in the gear shed for a while. The chainsaw probably needed sharpening. A bear. What a way to go. He couldn't focus on the saw, and after a while he just sat at the workbench, trying to imagine how it might have happened. One less person looking to collect. Thad couldn't say he felt bad about that.

THE NEXT MORNING THAD EMERGED FROM THE HOUSE with a cup of coffee, and the sight of three state police cruisers nosing down the driveway stopped him cold. When they saw him, they hit their lights and squawked their sirens. He sat down on the step with his hands splayed open beside him.

It took a few moments for them to establish the fact that he wasn't Hazen. There were two younger cops and one older. Their guns weren't drawn, but they talked to him with their hands resting on the butts of their pistols. The older cop checked Thad's ID. Sacajawea came out, and she and Thad sat on the porch with one officer watching them while the other two went through the house room by room.

"I told you, he's not here and I haven't seen him in two days," Thad said.

The cop nodded. "I know. Still have to check." After they'd searched to their satisfaction, the older cop asked Thad to come into the station. "You don't have to," he said. "But I'd really appreciate it if you would. We're trying to figure out what kind of deal we have going on here."

Thad rode with the older cop. Thad thought he would ask him questions on the way to the station, but he didn't. They put him in a small room with a desk and a chair in the middle of it. A watercooler and a coffee maker in the corner. A man came in and introduced himself. A detective. He was short, wearing a sport coat and tie, dark jeans. A sandy-colored goatee. Thad was trying to find his face familiar in some way. Him, or the three cops. These men lived in this town apparently, and Thad, to his recollection, had never seen them before in his life. He was unsure how that could even be possible.

The detective sat down and laced his hands in front of the table and thanked Thad for coming in. "We're just trying to figure out this situation," he said. "A man gets killed by a grizzly apparently, his daughter goes missing, and at some point in the last day or so, your brother was seen with her."

"What? Where?"

"They were seen at the Dippy Whip. Yesterday midmorning."

"At the Dippy Whip?"

"Correct. Eating ice cream cones. Several people saw them, and apparently it was memorable because they all reported the same basic thing. Hazen and the girl were there, and they had ice cream, and it didn't look like the girl was enjoying hers. She was crying. And then they left. At this point, our first objective is locating the girl. We're just trying to piece this thing together."

The detective asked Thad if he knew where Hazen might be. Thad said he really had no idea. He'd just gotten his first car; he could be anywhere. The detective nodded. Then he said, "What kind of man is your brother?"

"He's good at some things, bad at other things. I don't know. It sometimes seems like the things that he's good at don't tend to be things that will get you ahead in life, in this day and age. If that makes sense."

The detective nodded and said, "Mm-hmm," as if it made perfect sense to him. He wrote something down.

"I've heard from other sources that the two of you are some kind of survivalists. Spend a lot of time in the backcountry. Living off the land. That sort of thing."

Thad looked at him blankly. "We have the house down the road here ten miles, on the river. We live in it. Electricity, indoor plumbing, and everything."

"OK. But am I right in assuming that your brother would be comfortable setting out into the wilderness alone? Could probably survive for a while?"

"Better than most, I guess."

"You said he just got his first car. He's twenty-seven, correct?"

"Yes."

"Most people do that a lot sooner."

"We're not made of money. We share a truck."

"So you spend a lot of time together? You're close? Looks like you work together. Self-employed? What do you all do for money?"

"We cut and sell firewood, mostly. Our father left us the house when he passed. We don't need a lot of money to get by. We kill our own meat. The truck is paid for. Hazen just got a job working for a dogsled guy. We used to spend a lot of time together. Less lately. I've been under the weather this winter."

The detective said "Mm-hmm" again like this was all crucial information. He made notes. He cleared his throat. "What is your brother like, with women?"

"Huh?"

"I mean, does he have a girlfriend, or girlfriends? Has he ever? That sort of thing."

"Jesus. He hasn't really had a girlfriend that I know of. We're just not around a lot of women. He's normal with women, as far as I know. I haven't had a girlfriend in the last few years myself. It's Montana. *Man*tana. We're in the woods a lot. There's not women just leaping out from behind the trees."

"OK. OK. He's normal with women." The detective put his notebook down and looked at Thad for a long moment before turning his gaze out the small window. "You seem like a normal guy, Thad. You know? That's how you come across to me. If you could just give it to me straight here, is your brother like you? Is he just a normal guy? Is he different? You know him better than anyone on earth, I'd assume. So if I could just get it straight from you here, it would give me a place to start as we begin trying to figure this thing out. You know what I'm getting at?"

Thad was feeling the anger rise. "What are you trying to say? I think you're barking up the wrong tree here."

The detective leaned forward in his chair and steepled his fingers on the desk in front of him. "What tree should I be barking up?"

Thad rubbed his face with his hands, shrugged.

The detective gave Thad his card. He told him not to go on any trips. He told him that the sheriff's office would have a presence at his house. "In these sorts of situations, the individual often returns to the places he knows the best. Needless to say, if your brother contacts you, you get a hold of me immediately."

By the time he got home, it was late. There was a light on in the kitchen, and Sacajawea was sitting at the table, a mug of tea cold in front of her. He sat heavily. She asked if he was hungry and he wasn't. She scrambled him some eggs anyway and he forced himself to eat. She had questions and he answered them. After doing the dishes, she reheated her tea and sat across from him, dunking her teabag. After a while she said, "I might know a place. I'm going to go tomorrow morning, early. Will you come with me?"

THAD COULDN'T SLEEP. AT DAWN HE ROSE AND BLEARILY laced his boots on the porch. Sacajawea was up and ready. She had a small backpack, her hair tied back. He drove them to the log mansion downstream of them. The one that had just been purchased by the CEO of the Seattle company, Anderson Logistics, the originator of the letter that had been traveling in his jeans pocket with him for days. There was no sign of life, and he parked off to the side of their long driveway where no one could see his truck from the road, and Sacajawea led him up a faint trail along the creek.

As they walked, she told him that before she was born her father had tried his hand at sheep ranching. He still had cattle, but he got a hundred head of white-faced rambouillet and wintered them in the bottomland along the river. In the early summer, he hired a man and they drove them up to the high pasture in the mountains. The first year the hired man stayed in a sheep tent they'd hauled up with a two-horse team. That fall, when they were driving the sheep back down to the river bottom for the winter, the horses spooked and took off down the mountain with the wagon attached. They veered off the trail into the timber and soon foundered in the rocks and downed trees. One of the horses shattered its leg and had to be shot. The wagon was broken to pieces. Sacajawea's father had to cut the uninjured horse from its tresses. He left the dead horse where it lay, still attached to the ruined wagon. The next spring, he decided to forgo the wagon, and he and his hired man built a small cabin on a ridge overlooking the winter pasture. It was simply made but solid. Peeled and stacked logs. A corrugated tin roof and a small potbellied stove that they'd packed in on mules. There was one window with a screen and no glass, wood shutters that could be pulled and locked from the inside. The hired man would live up in the cabin for the whole summer. Fending off the coyotes and wolves and bears that came too close.

Sacajawea said that eventually her father got fed up with sheep—the shearing, the extra help he had to hire. He sold off the animals, and then as a part of the gradual shrinking of the ranch he sold the upper pasture, as well as the land below it, all the way down to the river. By the time Sacajawea was old enough to ride, the land no longer belonged to them, but whoever bought it did so as an investment property and never visited or made any sort of attempt to build, so she had free rein. When she came across the old shepherd cabin it became her place. She brought a tablecloth for the split-log table. She boiled water on the woodstove for tea and drank it sitting on the single front step overlooking the high meadow scattered with late-blooming mountain flowers.

She said she'd brought Hazen here once when he was young. It was soon after she'd come back for the summer, and Thad had been mad, ignoring her. She'd asked if he wanted to go on a hike and he'd said no. He went and helped his father in the woods. Hazen had gone with her. Never said a word about the place all these years. Thad could hardly believe it. In the grand scheme of things, a brother keeping the existence of a cabin secret from you wasn't a big deal, but Thad also knew that had the roles been reversed, he'd have told Hazen at some point. It was indicative of something, this surprising ability to harbor a secret. It also implied some sort of congress between Sacajawea and his brother. One that extended back into their childhoods and excluded him.

The trail was dry at first. As they gained elevation, it got wetter; at some points the creek was running right through it. It was steep, small noisy cascades dropping over the stones. They reached a ridge, and Thad had to stop and breathe, hands on his knees. It was the most exertion he'd had in months, and his head felt like it was going to float off his shoulders. While he rested, Sacajawea pointed out the place where her father had put the injured horse down. Even after all these years, some of the animal's remains had persisted, a scatter of dense, massive bones, dried and cracked with age.

They hit snow as they climbed the ridgeline. They postholed, and at one point Thad stopped to hurl the contents of his stomach. The cup of coffee he'd had this morning, the remnants of the eggs from last night, a brown gruel on the snow.

From up here they could see the stand of cottonwoods that hid their house. The river was a gray ribbon dividing sections of pastureland. The trail was covered by snow, but every so often there was a cairn of rocks. Spotted with rusty-orange and green lichen, they'd remained in the same spot, unchanged since Sacajawea's father had built them. Just stacks of flat rocks, knee-high. Nothing much, Thad thought, yet they'd lasted all these years. Left undisturbed, they might remain for centuries. Magpies would perch upon them, goats might rub against them, snow would cover them and then melt away. There were cities, whole civilizations that might not endure as long. It was strange to think that these markers, hastily assembled, might long outlast all the serious endeavors of a man's life.

They followed the cairns across a high meadow, and the trail got rocky and steep, scree shifting under their feet. Eventually Thad spotted the cabin from a distance; it stood out starkly against the snow. Solid and small. The chinking between the logs was black and peeling. The stovepipe was rusty, bent at a severe angle. He was surprised he'd never noticed it before. All his years of hiking around in these hills, and there were still places he'd never seen. There were tracks in the snow around the cabin. A thin line of smoke coming from the chimney pipe.

The girl was there. She was lying in bed, wrapped in a blanket, and she sat up suddenly, her eyes wide when Thad opened the door. Sacajawea motioned him out. She went in and shut the door behind her. Thad sat on a large spruce round that had been used as a chopping block. He leaned against the rough side of the cabin and had the sun on his face. He could hear the murmur of Sacajawea's voice and occasionally the girl's, but he couldn't hear what was being said. He knew Hazen wasn't here, and he felt a tendril of relief, if he was being honest with himself. The snow was coming out of the hills quickly with the recent warmth. The low-level trails would be mud bogs, the high country a mix of deep packed snow and open ground. The sun was good on his face and he closed his eyes, thinking of all the places Hazen might go.

THAD HAD A HARD TIME CONVINCING THE DETECTIVE that he wasn't withholding information about the cabin or Hazen's general whereabouts. The detective called Sacajawea in, and she answered his questions with the sort of dazed vagueness that Thad had come to realize she could easily summon if needed. The detective wasn't a stupid man, and he understood fairly rapidly that Sacajawea under interrogation was not a winning proposition for anyone.

Thad was forced to lead the detective and several other officers up to the cabin. Even though he told them repeatedly that Hazen was long gone, the detective and all the officers had their service revolvers, as well as bear-spray canisters attached to their belts. Even in his rather reduced physical capacity, Thad led the way. He had to stop several times to let the men catch up. When they neared the cabin, they motioned him back and drew their guns, assembling in some sort of official formation, two officers going around the back. The detective kicked the door for a dramatic entrance, but it was well-made, and quite solid, with a large wooden rotating latch on a bolt. The door didn't budge, so the detective was forced to spin the latch and enter in the traditional manner. The cabin was empty. No signs of occupancy since Thad's last visit. The officers wandered around the area, looking for clues, and Thad sat on the front step. The hikes over the last couple days had done something to clear his head. From here he could see the jagged white peaks of the Absarokas stretching all the way back into the park, where they linked with the Beartooths. An immensity of country. Lots of room out there for Hazen to roam. One officer was wandering around the edge of the timber. He had one hand on his pistol, one hand on his bear spray. He had a bear bell tied to his shoelace, and it jangled faintly as he walked.

Several days after the return trip to the cabin, the detective called Thad in. They'd questioned the girl extensively. There were no signs that anything untoward had happened to her during her time with Hazen. That's the word the detective used. *Untoward.*

"I told you," Thad said.

The detective shrugged. "Most often when something walks like a horse, and looks like a horse, it's not a zebra. You know?"

"I have no idea."

"She didn't have much to give us. Apparently, she came outside and she bumped into Hazen running around the side of the house. He saw her and was surprised and grabbed her arm and put her in his Subaru. They drove around for a while. She said his car smelled really bad. They went to the Dippy Whip and then the grocery store, and then they hiked up to the cabin. He left her with food and told her that someone would be up to get her before too long. He started a fire in the stove and then left. And that's it." The detective sighed and leaned back in his chair. When he'd gotten up to let Thad in, Thad had noticed a wince, a stiffness to his movements. He was still sore from the hike. "This may be neither here nor there, but this girl is like a ghost. She's got no ID. She's not on any register that I can find. Doesn't have a social security card. She says she's nineteen and won't tell us where she's from, or if that man was even her father. According to everything I've been able to dig up on him, he is unmarried with no dependents. None of it makes sense. Another thing," the detective continued. "We got the autopsy results back from the coroner. The bear got after him pretty good, mostly in the midsection area and thigh. Cause of death, however, was a single .22 bullet entering the back of the head at close range. The bear came along after. There were bagpipes near the scene. I'm guessing he was playing the instrument, didn't hear Hazen coming, and that was that."

"Could be."

"Here's the deal. You've explained to me the history you have with this man. The threats, the bad blood. And then there's Hazen's reality—his condition maybe? Has he ever taken an IQ test? What I'm saying is, there's no reason for him to go down hard for this if he comes in. There's lots of ways this could go. If you could reach out to him, I think there's plenty of ways that this could be not so bad."

"I have no way to get a hold of him. I've told you that a million times."

"OK. Sure. We're looking at a murder here, now. It's no longer just a kidnapping. And so there's going to be more people involved. Feds. They're going to consider Hazen armed and extremely dangerous, and they're going to go after him. If you could get a message to him perhaps, tell him what I just told you. Things would probably go easier for him."

"I wish I could," Thad said. "I have absolutely no idea where he is, or where he might be going. I have nothing for you."

Over the coming weeks, Thad would explain that he didn't know where Hazen was, countless times, to numerous different law enforcement agents. Soon there was a full-blown manhunt underway, helicopters, searchers on foot, dogs. Thad disconnected his landline and turned off the voicemail on his cell phone. TV people were trying to get a hold of him. Several showed up at the house and he started locking the chain gate, even when he was at home. He stayed in the house most of the time. Just going into town was unbearable. People's eyes on him constantly. He sat on the porch, and the evenings were interminable. Guilt, an itchy wool blanket drawn around his shoulders.

IT WAS UNSEASONABLY WARM THAT SPRING, AND THE snow came out of the hills in a hurry. The river raged and then subsided, and soon the backcountry was dry as tinder and the fires started. There were occasional reports of Hazen sightings. A hiker saw a man that fit his description near the Grand Canyon of the Yellowstone. A shed hunter reportedly saw him at the upper end of the Beartooth Plateau. Law enforcement press releases hinted at credible leads, but search efforts were stymied by the wildfires raging across the region.

The whole valley was socked in with smoke, the sunsets apocalyptic red. The investigation seemed to lose steam, and days went by where no law enforcement agent contacted Thad. Then a week, and then two. One morning Thad couldn't bear the thought of sitting around the house for one more moment. He loaded a pack and put on his boots and told Sacajawea he was going camping for a while and set out from right behind the house.

He wandered for over two weeks. He had a sort of mental list of places he wanted to check, and he made his way to most of them. The smoke burned his lungs at first, but then he got accustomed to it. Five days in he found his legs and his breathing came regular and strong, and sometimes he hiked all day for the simple pleasure of walking. At night the glow of fire made the ridges appear molten and alive. He saw hot spots blow up, balls of orange fire shooting up and reforming new blazes wherever they landed. Fires made their own wind and he didn't sleep well, anxious for a shift that would send the conflagration his way faster than he could move. There was no one out here looking for Hazen now; he knew that. And maybe Hazen had figured that out too. Maybe he'd started the fires to get people off his trail. It seemed possible. It also seemed possible that, in doing this, he could have gotten caught up. It was one thing to light a tree on fire in the middle of winter, or even in the early season damp. A wildfire in the heat of summer was not something you could outpace, or outthink even. It just came up and devoured you, and that was it.

Thad covered ground, soaking in cold creeks when the heat got to him, dodging the fires. He saw not one single sign of his brother's presence in any of the places he thought he might. In several of the areas there remained nothing but the blackened spires of lodgepoles, sharp and bare as knitting needles. Thad kicked his way through the smoking ash and tried to shake visions of Hazen burning alive.

Thad's father had been somewhat of a history buff. He'd told them that the Absaroka Mountains were named after the Crow people who'd once counted the valley as part of their vast hunting range. Absaroka meant "children of the large-beaked bird." He told Thad and Hazen that sometimes young Crow men, seeking some sort of direction, a vision for their life's purpose, would take to the mountains, climb a certain sacred peak, and make a bed of spruce boughs. There they would tend a small fire and fast, waiting on a sign from their gods. Sometimes, in order to gain the gods' favor, acts of blood sacrifice were made, cuts on the arm, a pinky finger hacked off at the second joint. Thad thought about this. He'd built a fire for coffee and he watched it, the wind off the larger wildfires licking his into strange sympathetic shapes. He didn't know what sort of favor he might expect. He didn't even know how to imagine the best desired outcome. Hazen finding his way home eventually, or Hazen peacefully dead? He wasn't Crow, and he had no gods who might grant him insight.

Finally, he went home.

ONE EVENING, THAD SHOWED SACAJAWEA THE LETTER. "That's a lot of money," she said.

"It is that for sure. Would make a lot of things easier."

"You'd still have to live somewhere," she said. "Where would you live?"

"I don't know. Buy a house in town, I guess. Buy a truck and camper and drive around for a while."

"It's your decision," she said. "Yours and Hazen's, I should say."

And in the end, that's what swayed him. He could imagine a scenario, however unlikely—Hazen still alive in a year or two, deciding to emerge from wherever he'd been hiding himself, coming down the valley and crossing the back pasture to find Thad gone. The place no longer theirs. He balled the letter and tossed it in the woodstove.

AS SUMMER MOVED INTO FALL, THAD STARTED HEADING into the mountains. His arm wasn't 100 percent, but he could still run the saw and it was much better than it had been. He had a feeling that this was how it was going to be from now on, this dull persistent ache. He could live with it. He felled and bucked, split and loaded the cut logs on his own, spending long days out on the Forest Service roads, his ears numb from the roar of the saw. The fires had subsided and there was a clarity to the air, and to his thoughts, that he had been missing for a long time. He sometimes had the feeling that he was being watched. On more than one occasion, he shut down the saw and yelled his brother's name.

HOME FROM A DAY IN THE WOODS, THAD WALKED UP the front steps, brushing the sawdust off his pant legs and sleeves, when he heard voices in the kitchen. Sacajawea talking to someone else sitting at the table. Thad froze when he saw the green stocking cap, the auburn braids. He was halfway across the threshold, and his first inkling was to turn, walk back down the porch, get in his truck, and drive away. But it was too late, and so he walked in and shut the door behind him. Sacajawea had finished with whatever she'd been saying, and they both sat there looking at him. Side-by-side there was something of a kinship in their postures if not their appearance. They shared a certain near-startled wideness to their eyes. No one said anything for a few moments, and then Sacajawea reached across the table and took the girl's hand. "Thad, this is Naomi," she said. "She came to see me in town today. She's going to stay with us for a while."

For lack of a better idea, Thad went to the sink and filled a glass of water. He drank it with his back to the women and then filled another. He couldn't think of anything to say, and so he walked to his room and shut the door.

He heard their voices, mostly Sacajawea's, in the kitchen until it was late. At one point there was the smell of toast, the brief whistle of the kettle. Eventually Thad fell asleep without having dinner or a shower, fully clothed on his bed.

He was up early, making coffee in the kitchen, when Sacajawea came in. She got a mug from the cabinet and put water on to boil. She leaned against the counter with her arms crossed over her chest watching him.

"She can't stay," he said.

"She's staying."

"I talked to the police about her. She's not his daughter. That's what they said. They don't know who the hell she is or where the hell she's from. God only knows. I don't want her here."

"She's staying."

"She's not staying. Where is she? Is she in Hazen's room? I'm dealing with this right now." Thad started to walk down the hall, and Sacajawea said his name sharp and quick and it stopped him cold. Just her voice. Somehow, he was eight years old again, fighting with his brother. She could always get them to separate by saying their names in that particular way. Names harder than slaps. Their father had never been able to do it like that. "Listen to me," she said. "You will not disturb her. She's sleeping." Thad turned, brushed by her, and found himself on the porch. Something was happening to him, a strange inability to fill his lungs with air; his breathing came fast and shallow, a warp and distortion at the edges of his vision. He stumbled to the truck, and he leaned on the tailgate with his hands on his knees, head down. There was a clear line of snot coming from his nose, and he spit and wiped at his face with his sleeve and spit again. There were tears, and he was coughing, tears and the snot was flowing, and he was damn near laughing because it had been so long he was doing a bad job of crying.

By the time Sacajawea came out, he'd composed himself and was sitting on the tailgate rubbing his face with his hands. "Mind if I sit?" she said. Thad could feel her gaze on him, but he didn't turn his head. A harrier hawk was working the field next to the driveway. It darted and swooped, scything low to the grass, hunting gophers. Thad watched it like it was the most interesting thing in the world.

He could smell the patchouli on her, her arm touching his, her leg touching his. Earl Grey steaming in her mug. They sat this way for a while, both of them looking off past the house toward the stand of cottonwoods and the river beyond.

Out across the field, the harrier dropped to the earth, talons first, wings thumping. It settled there, partially obscured by grass, ripping at something with its beak. Thad heard the front door open, and the girl emerged from the house, blinking in the sun. She sat on the front porch step and gave them a small wave. "I always thought I'd have a daughter someday," Sacajawea said quietly. "Your father made sure I'd never get one from him. But still, I always felt so sure that I would, somehow. I think that everything in the universe started as a single perfectly smooth thing that somehow broke apart. Everything that has happened since is just the pieces bouncing off one another in space. It's random, but occasionally broken pieces find themselves sticking together, and if this occurs an infinite number of times, don't you think that at some point everything will be one big smooth piece again?"

THE GIRL LIKED COFFEE. SOMETIMES THAD WOULD BE on the porch in the morning with a cup and she would come out. She never sat on the chair next to him, always on the step. They didn't say much. They drank coffee and looked out across the low hills and the farther peaks layered in the distance.

Once, Thad broke the silence to ask her if she'd brought her bagpipes with her. She shook her head. "I put them in the woodstove," she said. On another occasion she asked him what his brother was like.

"You met him," Thad said. "That's what he's like."

"What do you mean?"

"The way he acts is how he is. That's how I would describe him. Some people can behave in certain ways that are against the grain of their actual makeup. Hazen is incapable of doing that, I think."

The girl nodded and blew on her coffee. "We were only together for about two hours," she said. "He never stopped moving once. He told me he loved me."

ONE AFTERNOON, INSTEAD OF GOING TO THE WOODS, Thad grabbed a handful of his ugly creations from the fly-tying desk and went out to fish for a couple hours behind the house. The cottonwoods were a riot of gold, and the peaks had a new dusting of snow, and as he strung up his rod, an elk cut loose a shrill bugle from somewhere across the river.

He didn't have much faith in his flies and fished for an hour with no luck. On what he told himself would be his last cast, a large fish intercepted his streamer on the swing and laid out a blistering run downstream before breaking him off. When this sort of thing happened to his father, he'd always say something like, *Goddamn, that thing is probably halfway to the Missouri by now.* His father and Hazen had always been more into fishing than Thad. And now, standing there with the current clutching cold around his calves, his freshly parted tippet whipping loosely in the breeze, he looked downstream and imagined that large brown trout with a full head of steam going all the way to the Missouri, to the Mississippi, to the Gulf of Mexico. And he was cursing, laughing. He reeled up. Done fishing for the afternoon, he went into the gear shed. In a lucky bit of oversight, the Park Service had neglected to confiscate the raft at the bridge. While Thad had been laid low, Hazen had hiked up the canyon and floated it out. He'd deflated it, rolled it up, and stashed it up behind a stack of coolers and their father's old dented aluminum canoe. Thad hadn't thought to check on it before, but he did now. It was gone.

That evening he dug up an old atlas and traced the route with his finger. The Yellowstone dumped into the Missouri across the border in North Dakota. From there the Missouri flowed slow and muddy to the Mississippi at Saint Louis. He could just about picture Hazen out there, bobbing around on a blue fourteen-foot raft, catching catfish and dodging freighters. He imagined him, one day, making a final stroke and pushing his way into the warm Gulf in New Orleans. By Thad's calculation, it was over two thousand miles. Hard to imagine that a flake of snow at the top of the highest peak in the Beartooths would end up all the way down there someday. Water like an unbroken electrical current. Water like a system of arteries and veins. A guy way up in the mountains could put his hand in the river and it was the same water—a connected stream of molecules—as that flowing down the Mississippi. Maybe, if your brother happened to be sticking his hand in that water at the same time, wherever he might be, there's a chance he might know that it was you, feel you giving him a riverine handshake, telling him he was a crazy son of a bitch. Telling him to keep going all the way.

IT WASN'T JUST THE MONEY, ALTHOUGH THAT WAS A factor. It was a certain sense of things undone. Maybe some sort of half-assed notion to honor his brother with the completion of a piece of work. Crisp mornings, glorious, sun-streaked afternoons. Thad spent three days scrambling the rough edge of the canyon. There were many places where the going along the edge was impassible, sheer cliffs and teetering rock slopes. He'd almost given up when, one afternoon, glassing, he spotted a small smear of blue down by the river on the opposite side of the canyon. It was the raft; he was sure of that. From his vantage point he could see only a small slice of the bow. If anything of the load remained, he wasn't sure.

He hiked out and at dawn the next day he came back to the river from a trailhead on the opposite side. He had a pack with a light jacket, a headlamp, a section of rope, a bag of jerky. He made his way to the floor of the canyon by scrambling down a small creek drainage, thoroughly soaking himself in the process. The sun was up but bringing no warmth yet, his jeans plastered to his legs, both squelching with every step. He boulder hopped for a half mile upstream. The river flowed narrow and deep here, the water jade green, a wet crockery smell from the slabs of fallen gneiss.

It was nearly noon when he climbed one last boulder and looked down to see the pale-blue raft pulled way up into a jumble of rocks—what remained of the raft anyway. It was now a flat mat of deflated rubber, a large tear visible down the aft tube. No antlers anywhere in sight. Thad slid down the boulder he was standing on and made his way to the remains of the boat. There was a long section of their climbing rope tied off to the D ring at the stern. The rope was trailing up the steep rocks on the canyon wall, the other side attached to something up there that Thad couldn't make out.

He sat on a flat piece of rock in the sun, and the stone at his back was warm. He leaned into it, eyes closed. He wasn't surprised at the state of the raft. He'd figured the odds of anything surviving the runoff were slim. Hazen, by himself, hadn't been able to haul the raft far enough up the slope, especially loaded with antlers. Thad figured Hazen had tied the boat off and scrambled up the canyon as far as he could to anchor it, hoping for the best. That's what Thad would have done if it were him. No doubt a tree had come downstream and ripped a hole in the raft and that was that.

He chewed a piece of jerky and rested. There were cut-throat rising in the slow pool in front of him. He watched their dark shapes torpedo up from the bottom to gulp the small cream-colored caddis that were doing their skittering death dance over the surface. Thad found a thin stick next to him and he broke off a small piece. He threw it in the water and almost immediately a cutthroat came to slash at it. He threw more pieces of the stick. Then he started with tiny pebbles, and this worked too—every time his offering met the water, a fish, or sometimes several, would move hurriedly to intercept it. There was a reason this fish had been caught to near extinction in many places. An innate gullibility. Maybe not gullibility, just an inability to fathom deceit. Thad had watched brown trout in the summer come for his dry fly slowly, mouths agape, only to turn at the last second and spook because something didn't look right. A suspicious fish, a brown trout. Could a fish be suspicious? Could a fish be gullible? Thad wasn't sure. But he sometimes felt that humans underestimated the degree to which personality could be found in the animal kingdom. Could a dog feel abandonment? Could a grizzly bear feel satisfaction? Hazen had told the girl he loved her. Was it true, and if so, what did it mean?

After a while he got to his feet and shouldered his pack. On his way past the raft, he stopped and tugged on the rope attached to the bow. It was fastened hard to something up there. It was a good climbing rope, no reason to leave it. He shucked his pack and untied Hazen's bowline knot from the D ring at the stern. The slope was steep and he used the rope, hand over hand, to help him on his way up. The rope was a fifty-footer, and Hazen had gone up most of the length. There was a small ledge, and Thad scrambled over the side. A lawn mower–sized boulder rested there, and the rope was wrapped around its circumference twice and tied off. Thad untied the knot and began coiling the rope, looping from elbow to palm. When the rope was gathered neatly, he made a few half hitches to secure it and tossed it down toward his pack.

Before making his way back down the slope, Thad stopped to take a piss. He was standing next to the boulder, and when he glanced down behind it, he was surprised to see a tarp. It was one of the ten-by-fifteen camo-print plastic sheets they'd packed in to help contain the antlers. This one was folded into a roughly four-foot square, each corner pinned in place by several pieces of fallen rock.

After zipping up, Thad moved the rocks aside and pulled away the tarp. The soil here was chalky, gray, volcanic, leftover from the last time the caldera blew. At some point in the recent past, a section of unstable earth had been brought downslope by rain or snowmelt. Under the tarp, a curved section of what looked like bone or horn was protruding from the ashy dirt. He began scooping the loose earth away, slow at first, then faster, not stopping even after splitting a fingernail on a rock, his heart starting to hammer. It was a skull, but it wasn't white like bone; it was a deep coppery brown. It wasn't until he came to an eye socket that he had a sense of what it was. It looked like a bison skull oversized to the point of unreality. When Thad tried to heft the thing, the weight was startling.

THAD DIDN'T BREATHE EASY UNTIL HE HAD THE SKULL stashed in the shed, rolled up in an old canvas wall tent. It had been an awkward, heavy load strapped to his pack, and he'd been on edge the whole time, ready to bolt off the trail if he came upon anyone.

He sat on the skull for weeks, trying to figure out what to do. He'd gone to the library to use the computer, and after some research online he was fairly certain what he'd found—what Hazen had found—the semi-fossilized head of something called a *Bison antiquus*. It was an ancient species, extinct since the Pleistocene era, some ten thousand years ago. They were much bigger than modern bison, could weigh thirty-five hundred pounds, and had large curving horns. Apparently, the horns themselves didn't make it to the fossil state. What looked like horns on the skull were actually just the conical bone caps at the bases of the horns.

In life, the beast's horns would have been massive and sweeping, several feet long.

Thad had no idea what to do with the find. It was in good condition, and he knew it was valuable. He figured there was at least a decent chance that it was extremely valuable. But it was hard to say because there were none for sale to get a comparison, that was the problem. You couldn't just list something that probably belonged in a museum on eBay, he knew that much.

ONE MORNING HE FOUND TWO BACKPACKS PLACED NEXT to the door. Sacajawea and Naomi sat at the kitchen table, dunking tea bags. They were going on a trip.

"I've never seen much of the South," Sacajawea said. "We've decided to just drive south until it starts to get hot. No set plan whatsoever. Naomi was talking about wanting to see New Orleans, and I thought that was a great idea. I've always wanted to go too. So, end goal: New Orleans. Other than that? We'll see."

Thad poured coffee and leaned against the counter. "New Orleans?" he said. "Why there?" He watched the girl, and her eyes gave him nothing, no flicker, no discernible change.

She shrugged. "Its nickname is the Big Easy," she said. "I've always wondered why that is."

Thad sipped his coffee. "You know anybody there?"

"How would I know anybody there? I've never been there."

"I think it's possible to know people in places you've never been."

"I don't see how."

"Maybe you knew someone here, and then that person moved there."

Naomi shook her head and lifted her mug to her lips. Before long, they drove away. They'd be back in a month, or two; that's what Sacajawea said as she gave him a hug.

Thad sat at the table with his coffee going cold. He'd been unable to ask the girl outright if she'd heard from him. He couldn't do it. To know that Hazen was out there, had been in touch with someone, and that someone was not him, it was an edge too raw. He thought about Naomi and Sacajawea on the road. Mile after mile in the van's plush captain's chairs. He tried to imagine their conversations. Clearly they shared something. He could only guess what Naomi's life had been like, way back in the hills in that spooky house with the Scot. Hazen had recognized it while Thad had been oblivious. Thad became aware of something for the first time, a feeling in his chest, a hard little kernel of pride for his brother.

He made another pot of coffee, and when it was done brewing the kitchen was quiet. He was alone there, and he figured that was how it would be for a long while. He realized for the first time that acute aloneness has something of a presence. His lonely was dark as a shadow, and it sat there drinking coffee with him, a silent companion.

FOR LACK OF A BETTER IDEA, THAD CONTINUED TO GO to the library to scroll through articles about the *Bison antiquus*. He wanted to know why they disappeared. As far as he could tell, there were at least several proposed theories. Possibly their demise was brought about by changing habitat or drought. Some thought maybe it was just a slow evolution into the modern bison, not a real extinction. Some people thought overhunting was the culprit. The early North Americans had regularly slaughtered them with stone spears and arrows and by herding them over steep cliffs. These Stone Age hunters were often referred to as the Clovis people, and reading this name jogged something in Thad's memory.

When he and Hazen were young, maybe seven or eight years old, their father had a job up in the Shields Valley at the base of the Crazy Mountains. A rich man up there with a big log home tucked into the timber had hired him to thin out the dense growth around the house and outbuildings to reduce the risk of fire. During these years, Thad and Hazen often accompanied their father to his jobs. They sometimes helped in whatever small capacity they could, fetching things, stacking small pieces of wood, but most often they were left to entertain themselves—throwing their knives at stumps, climbing trees, wandering.

This job was memorable because at one point, when their father was nearing completion, the homeowner invited them in at the end of the workday. Near as Thad could remember, the man was their father's age, pale with dark hair and rimless glasses. He offered them Cokes, their father a beer. The Cokes were in glass bottles. Thad had never seen it that way before. The man spoke to their father about the job, and then he said he had something the boys might be interested in seeing. He led them down into the basement to a large room. The room was painted flat white and had floor-to-ceiling shelving, and the shelves were crammed with artifacts. There were displays of arrowheads, carved masks adorned with lank twists of horse hair, skeletons of strange animals, snakeskins, beaded moccasins, bows and arrows, rattles and shields. "I'm a bit of a collector," the man said. "Have a look around."

Thad and Hazen wandered, slack-jawed, in front of the shelves. Their father warned them not to touch anything. There was something on display in a glass case in the center of the room, and Thad found himself drawn to it. Under the glass was a wooden table, and nestled into a piece of black cloth on the table's top were bones, tiny human bones. A miniscule skull, arm bones, leg bones, pieces of a hand, everything a deep copper brown.

The man, seeing where Thad's attention had turned, came over and stood beside him. "I see you found my boy. How about that, eh?" he said. Thad's father and Hazen had come over, and they all stared while the man told them what it was and how he'd come to own it.

Apparently, the property was a place of some archaeological fame. At this point Thad couldn't remember all the details, but a member of the original ranching family to own the land had stumbled across a spearpoint covered in a red paint, called *ocher*, that had fallen out of an eroding hillside. Eventually many more artifacts were found, as well as the bones of a child. It was determined that this had been a burial site of the Clovis people.

In addition to being incredibly wealthy, the man who'd hired their father was somewhat of an amateur student of early American history. He sought out the property in large part because of what was found there. When he finally bought the land from the family who'd owned if for generations, one of the terms of the sale was that he got to keep what the house contained. Over the years, many of the artifacts found at the site had ended up in museums, but somehow, the remains of the child had remained under glass in the basement room. At the time, Thad had been too young to have much of an opinion on the matter; the bones were an oddity in a room jammed full of oddities. He did remember his father on the way home, shaking his head, saying the bones should be back in the ground or in a museum, not in some rich guy's basement.

After a little searching, Thad found an article on the Clovis people that referenced a burial location in Montana, in the Shields Valley. The bones found were those of an infant boy, and, in archaeological circles, these remains were referred to as Anzick-1. These were the bones Thad had seen all those years ago, he was sure of it. Apparently, the original ranching family who'd owned the land were named Anzick. To this day the remains were in a private collection, although the owner had allowed access to scientists. According to experts, the bones were thought to be somewhere between ten and twelve thousand years old, making this indeed the oldest-known burial location in North America of the Clovis people. The ocher was ceremonial, the site a place of obvious ritual.

The article had drawings, an artist's rendering of what the Clovis might have looked like—long dark hair, severe cheekbones. They were a nomadic people who moved across the plains of prehistory hunting camels, mammoths, giant bison, sloths, and horses, and maybe in turn being hunted by dire wolves, short-faced bears, saber-toothed cats—animals all gone now except for in those dimly lit areas of collective human memory, the taste of forgotten meat, the long teeth of nightmares.

It had been over twenty years since Thad had been in that man's basement. He wondered if the guy was still alive.

ON A SUSPICIOUSLY WARM DAY IN EARLY NOVEMBER, Thad took a drive. He headed up through the fizzled-out speed-trap towns of the Shields Valley. In the distance, the peaks of the Crazy Mountains only held thin ribbons of snow in the shadowed north-facing slopes. The valley unfurled in front of him, an expansive patchwork. The irrigated alfalfa fields still held the green of summer long after the last cutting. He hadn't been up there in a while, but he found the driveway without too much trouble. There was a log arch over the entryway, a weathered set of elk antlers mounted there. The house was at the base of a small hill. Even from afar, it was as massive a structure as he remembered. There were three stone chimneys. A cedar shake roof with copper flashing on the peaks and valleys. The long driveway was lined with Lombardy poplars, a precise regiment, bare limbs straight as soldiers at salute. Thad parked on the side of the circle drive and stood for a moment at the base of the flagstone front steps. There was a new F-350 parked there, a side-by-side with off-road tires next to that.

Thad rang the bell, and after a while the door opened. It was the same man who'd hired Thad's father all those years ago. Grayer, more stooped, still pale, wearing glasses, dirty jeans, and a wool sweater, moccasins on his feet with elk ivories as decoration dangling from the laces. The man looked at Thad with eyes slightly narrowed and said nothing.

Thad was surprised to find that a man with a house this large answered his own door. He'd been prepared for something else. Staff. A wife, maybe. Thad cleared his throat.

"Hi. You probably don't remember me, but I was up here a long time ago as a kid. You hired my old man to thin out some timber behind the house. My brother and I came up here with him. You showed us your basement. I'm Thad."

The man's brow furrowed behind his glasses. Then he smiled. He said his name was Lewis, and he invited Thad in. The kitchen was cavernous, a rough-milled wood floor with saw marks still visible, slate countertops, a massive gas range, a stainless steel refrigerator-freezer combo large enough to hang a side of beef. There was a stacked stone fireplace, and in front of it was a small round table and two wooden chairs. Lewis motioned for Thad to sit. He came back with two mugs of coffee.

"How long's this Indian summer going to last? This fall has been a miracle."

"It has been nice," Thad said. "Not much wind even."

"I was telling my manager, Nelson, the same thing this morning. This has been the calmest fall I can remember in years. For some reason it makes me think winter is going to come down with extra vengeance. We're on borrowed time here. Call me pessimistic. But you never know with the weather these days."

"You never do."

There was a moment of silence while they sipped the coffee. "How's your father?" Lewis said.

"He isn't."

"I'm sorry to hear that. Recently?"

"A few years ago."

"I never knew him well, but from what I could tell he was a good man. Hard worker. And your brother? What's his name? Something unusual."

"Hazen."

Lewis snapped his fingers and put his mug down. "Goddamn it, that's right. I'm sorry, but that whole deal was in the papers. I didn't put it together until right now. Jesus. I'd say you've had a hard go of it lately."

Thad looked into his coffee, swirled it around, and shrugged. "I'm not up here to talk about that."

Lewis held up his hands. "No, no need to explain. I'm sorry. I'm naturally curious. Nosy as an old woman, according to my ex-wife." He tapped a fingernail on the side of his mug. "What can I do for you, Thad?"

"I remembered you from when I was a kid. Your collection of stuff. I guess it made an impression on me. You still have it?"

"More than ever, I'm afraid. It's a bit of an obsession."

"I came up here because I was out walking the other day and I found something. I was wondering if you'd want to see it."

Lewis laced his fingers behind his head and leaned back, eyes squinted shut, laughing a strange, silent, convulsive laugh. The laugh continued, longer than seemed necessary.

"What?"

"It's nothing. Just that turn of phrase. You had to use that exact one."

"What one?"

"'I was out walking and I found something.' In Spanish, I believe it's *caminar es atesorar*. It means 'to walk is to gather treasure.' It's a perfect phrase. It contains the history of humankind. What else is there, really?"

"I don't know." Thad would have been happy to leave it at that, but Lewis sat there expectantly, clearly hoping Thad was going to disagree with him. "I guess I'll have to think about it. You want to see what I got, or not? It's out in the truck."

Lewis clapped his hands together and rose. They went outside.

It was a strange transaction. Initially it seemed that Lewis didn't want to buy the skull. He said as much. "It's breathtaking," he said. "But I can't. It really is magnificent though. I wonder where you came across it. Of course, I won't ask. Did you know these are the most common herbivores found in the La Brea tarpits? I've never seen one up close like this. Just reproductions. In museums. What a creature. Of course, I don't want it, I don't need it." He ran his fingers over the smooth ends of the horn caps, eyes closed. "Jesus. OK, I'll take it. Do you think there was more there, or was this it?"

Thad didn't understand what was going on with the man. It was on his face, as if he was in pain or being compelled by forces out of his control. If Thad wasn't mistaken, something verging on self-disgust there, too.

When Thad helped Lewis carry the skull to the basement, things started to make more sense. In Thad's memory, the room had been crowded with artifacts but well organized, even meticulously so. Thad didn't know much about museums, but in his memory the arrangement of Lewis's basement seemed to display the touch of a professional. However, clearly something had happened over the past twenty years.

At this point, there was barely a pretense of order. Thad's eyes seemed unable to find a coherent place to rest. The room was packed, to the ceiling in some places, with an obscene miscellany of artifacts. There was a sloping heap of beaded leatherwork: moccasins, fringed leggings, shirts, ornate pieces of tack, rawhide saddles, headbands. There was a complete suit of tanned buckskin, tunic and leggings, every inch adorned by an intricate pattern of flattened and dyed porcupine quills. There was another, separate, slightly smaller pile of headdresses, a massive avian deconstruction, plumage of every imaginable size, color, and configuration looking for all the world like the remnants of some massive prehistoric bird that had been picked to pieces by a truly colossal predator. There were plastic bins bristling with spears, polished atlatls, hatchets of flint and hammered brass, coupsticks painted in lurid hues, unstrung bows decorated with strips of pure-white ermine. Oddly balanced fetishes of polished petrified wood and brass and bone hung on gutstrings from the ceiling alongside dream catchers in an absurd variety of size and specificity, enough dream catchers to snare every dream that had ever been dreamed from humanity's dawn.

Lewis directed Thad to put the skull on a wooden stool next to a stack of bison-hide shields and what looked like a fossilized femur of some large animal Thad couldn't identify. Lewis looked around and rubbed his hands together briskly. "Excuse the mess," he said. "I'm in the middle of a bit of a reorganization. You wouldn't believe the amount of work that goes into maintaining a collection like this. I sold a company and retired at age forty-two. Since then, I've worked harder right here than I ever did then. I'm divorced and I have no children, and now this is how I spend my time. A life's work."

Thad jammed his hands into the pockets of his jeans. He wanted to leave. The basement was making him claustrophobic. He wanted his money, and then he wanted to leave. But Lewis was gesturing that he should stay a while, look around.

"You still have those bones?" Thad said.

"The boy? Of course. That boy got this whole ball rolling. It's an important piece in the puzzle of human history. Made an impression on you, did it?"

"I remember it. That's all."

Lewis laced his fingers together and made a steeple to crack his knuckles. "I've got something you might be interested in seeing. It's a new acquisition. Came up from Texas. I haven't shown it to many people. It cost me a small fortune, but the minute I saw it I knew I had to have it in my possession. There was no way I could just let it *circulate*."

Lewis led Thad through the maze of artifacts to the center of the room, to the glass containing the remains of Anzick-1, one of the only relatively uncluttered flat surfaces in the whole place. On the case was a small black velveteen container the size of a tissue box. Lewis removed the top and presented the box to Thad with a flourish.

At first Thad was unsure what he was looking at. Realization dawned on him slowly, and hard on its heels came revulsion. He handed the box back to Lewis.

"You know what that is?"

"I know what it is."

"Have you ever seen one in real life before?"

"Hell no."

"I got that from a man who came all the way up from Texas just to show it to me. Have you ever heard of a group of people called the Comancheros?"

Thad shook his head. He found himself wiping his hands on his Carhartts, as if just holding the box had somehow transferred to his skin the essence of what it contained.

"They were an interesting bunch. They operated down there in West Texas and New Mexico. They were mixed, not full Indians, not totally Mexicans either. They traded with the Comanches, and that's how they got their name. They'd set out for Comanche country with blankets and beads and whiskey, probably guns too, and they'd barter for hides, horses, and the other thing the

Comanche were known for holding: slaves. The man I bought this particular piece from told me that it had belonged to the men of his family for generations. By tradition, the oldest son passed it down to his oldest son. Until him. He had only a single daughter. He told me he could have passed it on to the son of his younger brother, but in truth, he was getting older and didn't want the weight of holding it anymore. He thought the family needed to get rid of it.

"Over the years they'd had more than their share of misfortune. His own father had been killed by a lunatic who, for no apparent reason, drove a semitruck into a café in Magdalena, New Mexico. His father had been there, eating breakfast before work, and the truck obliterated him against the café bar. His father's father had drowned in a small boat while fishing on a day when there had been not a breath of wind or a hint of wave. There'd been sickness and lost fortunes. One of his uncles had won the New Mexico Powerball lottery. Before he could go claim his millions, he stopped at a bar to get a celebratory drink, and during this drink, only one drink, his car was stolen and never recovered. The lottery ticket had been tucked in the sun visor. The man was fed up. He needed to rid his family of this curse. He said he was going to use the money to pay his daughter's college tuition. I was glad I could help. If you're wondering whether I'm nervous to have something like this, the answer is no. It's not that I discredit this man's superstitions; in fact I think a curse can be a real thing, but it only works if you believe in it, if that makes sense. A curse is nothing more than an evil placebo.

"When it comes down to it, I feel that I need to house these things, buy them from people and keep them, as a service. It's a burden. It didn't start out that way, but that is what this whole thing has become. I sold a company at age forty-two. And now this is my life's work. I've become a depository. A storehouse of ancient American history." Lewis spread his arms as if he was trying to bring the hideous variety into himself.

Driving home, Thad stuffed the roll of hundreds in his jacket pocket, and he rested his hand there. More money than he'd ever had in his possession at one time. A staggering sum that had yet to begin to feel real. He thought that Lewis might actually be insane. The man had the bones of an ancient child in his basement. If that wasn't enough, now he had that hank of long strawberry-blond human hair. The hair had been braided, all the way up to the leathery piece of tanned skin to which it was still attached. A scalp. The braid was held together by a faded red velveteen ribbon, tied in a bow.

THE DAY THE KENYON NOBLE TRUCK SHOWED UP WITH the shingles and a lift to get them up to the roof, Thad dug his father's old tool belt out of the shed. When the boys were young, their father had worked on and off as a framer in Big Sky, and by now the belt had to be at least thirty years old. It had been made at a local tack shop out of bison hide. The nail pouches were thick waxed canvas. It was brass riveted and heavy, but after thirty years it just looked nicely broken in. Thad strapped the belt around his waist. The hole he passed the buckle post through must have been the exact one his father had preferred because it was worn and ovaloid from use. The belt and the weight of the tools that hung from it settled comfortably around his waist, as if it had been made for him. He climbed the ladder and got to work.

He'd rented a nail gun and compressor, and the staccato sound of his firing rose above the constant drone of the generator. He fell into a steady rhythm, and by the time he broke for lunch he was feeling good about his progress. After making a sandwich, he climbed the ladder back up to the roof to eat it, straddling the ridgeline. A good view from up there: he could see the river until the point at which it disappeared into the canyon, the Absarokas stretching back all the way to the eternal winter of the Beartooth Plateau. In one of the last conversations Thad had with his father, before his death, his father had told him that he wasn't much scared of what was coming next. He said that, as far as he knew, 100 percent of the folks who died preferred to stay that way. Death had a perfect record. Not one unhappy customer. It couldn't be that bad. He'd also said that raising the two of them had been the very best thing he'd ever done. He said that no matter what happens between a man and a woman, it's impossible to regret having children. He said that life can pass you by but having a family is how you make positive the passage of time, how you add resonance to your years.

At the time, it was hard for Thad to fathom, but now, living in an empty house set on the edge of an empty country, he could see where his father had been coming from. Thad finished his sandwich and wiped the mustard from his fingers on his jeans. The first step was a roof that didn't leak. After that, who knew? It was Friday night; probably they had a live band at the Goose. Maybe after work he'd put on a clean shirt and head down. Maybe if the band played a Haggard cover, he'd ask a woman to dance. He'd endured Mrs. Tronsen's two-step lessons in freshman-year homeroom, same as everyone else. It had been a while, but he could hold his own.

ABOUT THE AUTHOR

Callan Wink is the author of the novel *August,* as well as a collection of short stories, *Dog Run Moon.* He has been awarded fellowships by the National Endowment for the Arts and Stanford University, where he was a Wallace Stegner Fellow. His stories and essays appear widely, including in *The New Yorker*, *Granta*, *Playboy*, *Men's Journal*, and *The Best American Short Stories Anthology.* He lives in Livingston, Montana, where he is a fly-fishing guide on the Yellowstone River.